TRENT REEDY

F

FRANCES LINCOLN
CHILDREN'S BOOKS

Text copyright © 2011 by Trent Reedy
Translations on pages 56, 121-2, 156, 214 and 253
copyright © 2011 by Scholastic Inc.
The right of Trent Reedy to be identified as the author of this work
has been asserted by him in accordance with the Copyright,
Designs and Patents Act, 1988 (United Kingdom).

First published by Arthur A Levine Books, an imprint of
Scholastic Inc., in 2011
First published in Great Britain in 2011 by
Frances Lincoln Children's Books, 4 Torriano Mews,
Torriano Avenue, London NW5 2RZ
www.franceslincoln.com

Excerpts from *Yusuf and Zulaikha* and *The Shahnameh* were newly translated
for this book by Roger Sedarat, a professor of poetry and translation
at Queens College in New York City. www.sedarat.com

A catalogue record for this book is available from the British Library.

ISBN 978-1-84780-271-2

Set in Palatino

Printed in Croydon, Surrey, UK by CPI Bookmarque Ltd. in July 2011

1 3 5 7 9 8 6 4 2

This book is dedicated to Katherine Paterson
who believed I should try to write it
even when I doubted if I could,
and to my father, Dan Reedy,
who told me to hold on to the dream.
I did it, old man.

1

I traced the letters in the dust with my finger, spelling out my name: *Zulaikha*. Squinting my eyes in this middle time between night and morning, I checked to make sure my brothers and sister were still sleeping. Then I began to write the alphabet. *Alif, be, pe, te...* What was the next letter?

I wriggled my fingers in the cool brown powder before I swept out what I'd written. "I'm sorry, Madar-jan," I whispered, hoping that somehow her spirit could hear me. "I'm forgetting what you taught me."

My sister, Zeynab, still slept on her toshak next to mine. Her shiny, straight black hair draped over her smooth, round face and her pretty mouth. She licked her lips in her sleep. No matter how many times I looked at her, I was always fascinated by her beauty, wishing I could be even half as pretty as she was. I found my blue chador and pulled it up over my face. It needed a wash, smelling of salt and smoke.

1

Roosters crowed, and a few dogs barked. The small city of An Daral still slept, but not for much longer.

"Allahu Akbar," came the voice of the muezzin over the speaker a few streets away, calling the faithful to prayer. The day had begun.

Zeynab rubbed her eyes. "Ooooh, so early." She turned to Khalid and Habib, who stirred on their toshaks. "I wish I was still young enough to stay sleeping."

I didn't say anything, but poured water from a pitcher into a tub to perform wudu' and cleanse myself for prayer. Zeynab did the same, and then we faced west on our rugs and went through our prayers, standing, bowing, sitting, and always giving thanks and praise to Allah the most merciful. This was the best prayer of the day. Soon Allah would bring the sun up behind us and touch us with its warmth.

After we rose from our prayer rugs, Zeynab went right back to her toshak to sleep. I never understood what she gained from maybe two minutes more of sleep time. I turned to watch the morning glow, the golden pink swell of light building behind the mountains to the east.

In the name of Allah the most merciful and his prophet

Muhammad, peace be upon him, I give thanks for this new day and ask help so that I can be a daughter my mother would have been proud of. So that I might be a blessing and not a burden to my father. Then I added as I always did, *And please grant me peace with Malehkah.*

With my personal prayers finished, I stepped over to my sister and gently shook her shoulder.

Zeynab groaned. "Come on, Zulaikha, just a bit longer. Malehkah hasn't even called for us yet."

I tugged her sleeve. "Like the muezzin says, prayer is better than sleep."

She yawned. "Maybe I pray in my sleep. In my dreams."

"You don't mean that," I said. "Anyway, Malehkah will already have the tea and rice ready. She'll be—"

"Zulaikha. Zeynab." Malehkah's sharp voice cut through the morning stillness and echoed off the compound walls. She did not like it when we kept her waiting. This was true.

"Zeynab," I said, though her name always sounded more like Zeynav when I said it. "Let's go."

I started for the stairs that led down into the house, but then I saw that my little brother Khalid had twisted out of his blankets. Even though he was nearly nine years old, he slept more restlessly than two-year-old Habib. When I moved his blanket up to cover him, he put his thumb in his mouth and reached for me with his other hand. I smiled and smoothed his hair as I pulled away.

"Go back to sleep, bacha," I whispered. "I'll have something for you to eat when you wake up."

Malehkah waited at the base of the stairs. "What took you so long getting down here? Zeynab, look after the rice." She nodded in my direction, her hands wrapped around her bulging stomach as if to protect her unborn baby from me. "Zulaikha, go and buy some naan. Hurry. Your father and Najibullah are hungry."

I pulled my chador up over my head, slipping the end around to cover my face. Malehkah didn't like looking at my mouth.

"Don't you be talking to any shop boys either. It will be hard enough trying to find a husband for you some day without people thinking you're too eager." My father's wife held out a dirty, wrinkled one-hundred Afghani note. "And bring back the extra money. Remember, thieves lose their hands."

"Yes, Madar." Even though I'd had to say this for years, it still hurt to refer to my father's second wife as mother, especially when she was being so mean. I'd never stolen in my life, and I certainly never said more than was necessary to any shopkeepers. It didn't matter. Whatever I did, Malehkah was always mad at me. Still, I had to try to please her, to prove to her that I wasn't so terrible, and to make peace in my father's house.

When my madar, my real mother, still lived, life with Malehkah was better. Or maybe I was just so young that everything seemed better. Madar-jan had been kind to Malehkah, helping her adjust to life with us and always placing the needs of the family ahead of her own. But I don't know how or why my mother had been so nice to her. I thought about what she always said whenever I was upset: "'Every triumph from patience springs, the happy herald of better things.'"

As I made my way across the front courtyard, I tried to open myself to everything around me. I felt the smooth, soft dust between my toes, and I listened to the sound of the breeze whispering and rattling through the palm leaves of our date tree. I noticed all the deep blues, greens, and reds painted onto the elaborate, metal double door at the front of our compound. I took in the old brown smell and the warmth of the thick mud-brick wall that protected us from everything outside. Madar-jan would have reminded me to be patient enough to forget all the ugliness and focus on these good things.

I turned around to look back at our house in the middle of the compound. It wasn't the nicest in An Daral, just a one-story mud-brick house with five rooms, but Baba had painted the outside a pretty shade of blue. I loved my home.

"Zulaikha!" Malehkah stepped out onto the porch.

"Bale!" I hurried to the outer wall and unlocked the small single door, careful not to cut my hands on the sharp bits of metal that poked out like teeth from the welds on the lock. Then I stepped out into the street. Out into the public world.

The night's coolness lingered in the low ruts of the bumpy, uneven road. But warm beams of sunlight shone down between the peaks of the mountains and branches of the trees overhead. I wiped my brow. When the day started this warm, the thick heat would bake everything by midday, forcing the men down to the café, where they'd sit drinking orange Zam Zam soda, talking, and watching the red line climb the thermometer almost to the very top. I walked quickly down the side of the road, wrinkling my nose at the stink of the sewage streams that trickled from the holes in the compound walls. But a little bad smell was better than walking out in the open, where someone might notice me.

Women passed me on the street, carrying naan in cloth bundles and chatting in low voices beneath their chadris. Malehkah had finally convinced Baba-jan that Zeynab was too old and too pretty to go outside the compound not covered up. When I had asked for a chadri too, Baba-jan just squeezed my shoulder, chuckled, and told me that I was too young. I was thirteen. I didn't feel young, not like my brother Khalid. And I saw the wrinkles in the corners of my father's eyes when he smiled at Zeynab in her new sky blue chadri. He looked very happy to see his daughter growing up. I wanted some of that smile for me too.

Just ahead was the door to the compound of one of the families in the Abdullah clan. I picked up my pace, crossing to the wall on the other side of the street and padding along as quietly as I could until I reached the river. At the best crossing place, the river was only ankle deep in summer, so I waded out and felt the cool water and the sand between my toes. Behind me, the road was empty and silent. I could relax for a moment.

At the bazaar on the east side of town, a few people already moved about their early business. A dented and rusted white pickup rattled along to deliver melons from Farah City. Big metal shutters rolled up to open stores, and shopkeepers brought their goods out for display in front of their stalls.

Everything was calm and quiet now, but that wouldn't last long. The day's first shoppers were already haggling over prices, the beginning of a blur of colors, smells, and sounds.

A donkey's loud bray echoed above all the noise. Soon, people would be in the street and on every corner, pausing only to trade in the day's gossip. Soon, there would be more people trying not to stare at my disfigured face. I pulled my chador over my mouth and hurried along to the naan shop.

"But what good will come of it? Answer me that." The owner of the bakery squatted, flopping a ball of dough onto the cement slab on the floor. He turned it, kneaded it, and flopped it again.

"It's freedom! We'll get to decide for ourselves who will rule us." A boy about Zeynab's age stoked the fire for the tandoor.

I shifted my weight and leaned against the counter at the window. If I were a man or even an older woman in a chadri, they wouldn't ignore me like this.

The shop owner and a very old man smoking a cigarette in the corner looked at each other and laughed. The owner added a sprinkle of water to his dough, kneaded it a little, and then spread the dough out in to a long oval. The warm smell wrapped around me, reminding me that it had been a long time since I'd last eaten.

"All that I decide for myself is how much naan to bake. This election they're so busy getting ready for. Parliament? A big American idea. And a bunch of criminal warlords running for office." He slapped his dough down hard. "Those rich Americans want to help me? Tell them to buy some naan! For now, I don't care who is in Kabul as long as they leave me alone." The owner spread out his dough and pointed at the boy and then at the oven.

"Excuse me, sahib," I said.

He almost burst with a sigh so big, one might think I'd been pestering him for a week. "What do you want?"

I had to let go of my chador to place the money on the counter. "Three pieces, please."

As soon as the man saw my mouth, he wrinkled

his nose in disgust. "Oh, it's you. Yes. Get her some naan, will you?" he said to the boy. I paid the boy, who kept his eyes fixed on the floor, on the naan he was placing in the cloth I'd laid out on the counter, on the change he gave back to me, on anything except me.

"There," said the owner. "Now go. You'll scare away my customers."

I turned and quickly walked away. Nobody was waiting behind me to buy the man's naan, but nobody wanted me near their shop for very long either. I was used to it. I left the bazaar as fast as I could.

By the time I crossed the river again and made my way back to the road, the golden smell from my bundle was making my stomach rumble. I walked faster because naan tasted best when fresh. It became tough and chewy very quickly. Also, Malehkah was waiting for my return. I quickened my pace to a rapid walk, not quite a run. I should have run on the way to the bakery. I'd taken too much time.

I passed a small wooden door on my right and heard muffled laughter. The door snapped shut before I could see who was there, but I knew who it had to be. I hurried up the road. Then I heard the door open again and footsteps behind me, quickly closing the gap. I started to run, doing my best to hold on to my bundle. I didn't want Anwar to know I was scared of him, but I didn't want him to hurt me either.

My toe hit a rock. I tripped and almost dropped the naan. That was all Anwar needed. He ran up ahead of me and blocked my way forward on the road while his cousins Omar and Salman blocked my way back. I took a step backward.

Anwar stepped closer. He was dressed in the loose-fitting pants and matching oversized shirt called a perahan-tunban. He also had on fine leather sandals and even a small hat with gold stitching and little round mirrors. His perfect smile would have been handsome if I didn't already know how mean he was. I looked for a way around him, but he followed my eyes and cut me off, moving even closer to me. Much too close.

"HEEEEE-HAAAAAAW!" Anwar dragged his sandal in the dirt like an angry bull. "Hey, Donkeyface! Where you going? Why you running?" he shouted. "I want to talk to you."

I backed away from him, pulling my chador over my mouth, but when I hit the wall I jerked and dropped my cover.

Anwar pretended to gag and acted like he was

11

throwing up. Omar put his hand to his mouth and pointed two fingers at me from under his nose, mocking me for the way my twisted teeth stuck straight forward from the gap in my split upper lip.

"HEEEEE-HAAAAAAW! HEE-HAW!" Salman shouted until his face was red.

"You so ugly, Donkeyface. Why don't you put on a chadri? Nobody wants to see your ugly mouth!" Anwar held a hand up to shield his eyes from my face.

"Leave me alone, Anwar," I shouted, but my words came out as crooked as my teeth.

I shouldn't have spoken. Omar and Salman launched into a cruel imitation of the way my cleft lip forced me to mispronounce words. But Anwar just smiled coldly and slowly stepped forward. I tried to make my legs stop shaking, but they felt as weak as soggy naan.

We stood like that for a moment. Omar galloped around in a circle and let out another long donkey call.

Suddenly, Anwar jerked back his hand to slap me. I flinched, almost dropping my food and turning my face away. But instead of hitting me, he tore a big chunk of naan from one of my pieces. Then he tore his piece to give some to Omar and Salman. I watched the other two grinning and chomping loudly with their mouths open, eating my family's food.

Before I even thought about it, I reached out and snapped the bread from Anwar's fingers before he could take a bite. "Thieves lose their hands!" I shouted at him.

Omar and Salman started to mock me again, but Anwar's eyes narrowed. He turned to his cousins. "Did you hear that? This ugly, donkey-faced *girl* is going to preach the law to us?" He spun round to face me. "My father is hajji! He has made the hajj to Mecca while yours hasn't even been to the Great Mosque in Herat!"

Now I was shaking terribly, and my stomach felt twisted and tight.

"You like being a little Talib? Preaching Taliban punishment? I'll give you what you like, Donkeyface. Stone you, Taliban style. Break those ugly teeth from your freak mouth." Anwar bent down to pick up a rock that was only slightly smaller than his fist.

It was my chance. As soon as he looked down, I stepped around him and ran, holding the naan tightly and moving as fast as I could.

If I kept running, maybe they'd get tired of chasing me and then leave me alone.

But I had only gone a few paces when the loud roar of an engine stopped me. The trees made it hard to see, but it looked like a man was coming around the curve ahead of me. He must have been a very tall man to be seen up over the wall.

Then an enormous tan car rounded the corner. It was so wide that there was less than a meter on either side between the car and the walls. On top was a big gun with a barrel like a cannon. What I had thought was a tall man was really only the top half of a soldier riding in the car, standing straight up through the roof of the vehicle behind the gun.

Soldiers! The man at the gun wore a huge helmet with black goggles strapped to the top. His chest was big and boxy with some sort of armor. I let my chador fall away from my face and cowered close to the wall.

But instead of firing the gun, the man sticking out the top of the big car smiled and waved. "*Salaam, rafiq!*" he shouted in a strange-sounding Dari as the car, or maybe it was really a truck, drove slowly by us. Another truck rounded the corner, but the man sticking out the top of that one was facing backward, with a gun that had a much longer, narrower barrel. When that man passed, he tilted back his tan helmet and shouted something in a language I didn't understand. His teeth flashed very white in the darkest face I'd ever seen.

"An African!" Omar pointed at the dark man.

All three boys were watching the soldiers go by, completely ignoring me. If the big trucks hadn't been coming from the direction I had to go, I would have escaped the moment the boys turned away. My legs shook, almost twitching with my eagerness to run.

The dark-skinned man had been smiling, but when he saw me, he frowned. Of course, most people who saw me frowned, but when such a look came from an armed soldier, it was even worse. I covered up my face with my chador.

The soldier shouted something down into his truck as he ducked under a tree branch. The big vehicles continued on down the road.

"It's the Americans!" Anwar clapped as he started to follow the gun trucks. "Give me radios! Soccer balls! Ball, ball, ball!" He turned to Salman and Omar. "Come on! They've got everything in those trucks!"

I pulled the naan up close to my chest and ran

toward home, hardly even dodging the big sharp pebbles. Just before I reached the next bend in the road, I risked a look back.

Thank Allah, the boys were running off after the trucks, clapping their hands and calling out. The American African soldier threw out a handful of something sparkling, and Anwar and his cousins scrambled in the dirt to pick it up. I watched until the vehicles passed another bend. When I couldn't see the soldiers riding above the tops of the walls, I ran.

Back in our compound, I closed the street door and leaned against the warm mud-brick wall. Home. Neither Anwar nor big scary soldiers would bother me here. Wiping the saliva that always came from my split upper lip whenever I ran, I tried to catch my breath enough to call for Zeynab. For Baba. Anyone. I had to tell everyone what I had just seen. They probably wouldn't believe me. Everyone had been saying that An Daral wasn't an important enough village. But they were wrong. The Americans had come to town!

2

"Baba-jan, Baba-jan!" I rushed into the house, barely closing the door behind me. Everyone was sitting on the floor ready to eat, the dishes laid out on the big cloth dastarkhan in the middle.

Malehkah had jumped at my shout as she poured my baba's tea. "Be quiet! Look what you made me do!" She grabbed a small towel and mopped up the spill.

"But I have to tell you—"

"I said quiet. Your father has a headache. And what took you so long getting back?"

Baba rubbed the bridge of his nose. My older brother, Najib, sitting next to him, looked like he would fall asleep any moment. They were always tired after welding most of the night. Zeynab looked up from peeling an orange for Khalid and Habib and offered me a piece. I shook my head and set down the naan, keeping the torn piece on the bottom.

"The Americans. They're here. In An Daral. They

drove right past me on the river road. They have these big trucks with guns and—"

"This is true?" Baba looked at me, instantly awake, his cup held halfway to his mouth.

"Bale, Baba."

Baba set his cup down and elbowed Najib. "What do you think, Najibullah?" My brother shrugged and looked like he was about to speak, but Baba continued. "It's worth a look maybe."

Malehkah sat down between her boys and put her arm around Habib. She smiled down at him when he leaned against her, chomping his piece of orange. Then she turned to me and all the joy fell from her face. "You stay away from those men, Zulaikha. I've heard terrible things about what those infidel soldiers do to Afghan girls, even to girls like you."

"They just drove past. I didn't—"

Baba held up his hand. "She's right. You need to stay away from those men." He tore off a piece of naan. "Hajji Abdullah was telling the truth. The Americans don't waste any time. They're here exactly when they told the hajji they'd be here."

"You knew they were coming, Baba-jan?" Zeynab asked.

"Hajji Abdullah came by the shop a few days

ago. He says the infidels have some crazy idea about building a new school. Want these buildings done in the modern style. He says those rich Americans will pay hundreds of thousands of Afghani for good welders."

"We already have a school," said Khalid.

Baba shrugged. "They say it's not big enough. Doesn't allow girls."

Girls? I stared at Baba. Zeynab spoke up. "But Baba-jan, girls don't even go to school. What good are all those books to a woman with a good husband?"

Malehkah smiled, but shook her head and looked down.

Baba waved us all silent. "Well, I agreed to hear them out. Let's just hope that everything the hajji says about American contracts is true. School for boys. School for girls. School for goats. Who cares as long as they pay?" Baba finished eating before he led Najib out of the house and the compound.

A school for girls? There'd never been such a thing in An Daral. What would it be like to go to school?

Malehkah discovered the piece of naan that Anwar had torn. She held it up. "Here." She peered at me over the gaping hole. "Zulaikha couldn't wait until she came home to start eating. You boys better get something while you still can." She struggled to stand up. "Make sure the boys eat. When you're done, Zulaikha, give them a bath. Then you have clothes to wash. Zeynab, the cow's stall needs to be cleaned out and that crack in the back section of the wall should be patched."

"Bale, Madar," Zeynab and I said together as Malehkah went back to the kitchen to start washing dishes.

"Hold still, Habib." Trying to wash my little brother was nearly as difficult for me as pronouncing his name. Sometimes I thought Malehkah gave him that name with all the tricky *b* sounds just to mock me. He wiggled around in our metal washtub out back by the well, always bending down to put his hands in the water or to play with soap bubbles. I twisted the rag to let the water pour onto the top of his head. How he made himself so dirty I didn't know, but the water ran off his head as if it hadn't even touched his thick, black mop of hair.

"Cold." Habib wiped his little hands over his face.

"I know, bacha. But can you be a big boy for your sister?"

Khalid went past us, dragging a piece of scrap

metal toward the back wall.

"What are you doing?" I asked him.

"Madar won't let me go outside." Khalid propped the metal against the fuel barrel in the back corner of the compound. "She says the soldiers are dangerous."

The fuel drum stood next to a crack in the wall. It would boost Khalid up to the crack, which he evidently meant to climb to get to the roof of the stable.

"Just stay down. Your mother is right. Those men are dangerous. And you're going to get hurt trying to climb up there."

"But I want to see!"

"Try the roof of the house," I said.

"I did." Khalid repositioned the metal.

Habib splashed his feet in the water, stepping up and down. He blew out a frustrated huff and shook his head.

"Okay, Habib. I'm sorry. Let's get you washed up." I dabbed the wet rag on his tiny button nose.

A shadow stretched across the concrete near the well. I straightened up and turned around to see Malehkah drop a bundle of clothes in a pile. Khalid conveniently turned into the perfect son for his mother, pulling a few weeds from the ground near the pomegranate bush.

"Hurry up with Habib. It shouldn't take that long to wash a two-year-old. Then wash these," she said. "And make sure you actually *clean* Khalid's and Habib's clothes this time."

"But I always—"

"Last time you only scrubbed your father's and Najibullah's clothes. My boys need clean clothes too."

"They're my brothers, Madar. I would never—"

"Just do it!" Malehkah turned back toward the house. "You must learn to stop arguing if we're ever going to find you a husband. And hurry! I want it done before your father gets home." She looked over at Khalid. "Watch him too. Make sure he stays inside while those soldiers are on the loose."

"Bale, Madar." I looked at the dirty clothes next to our old washboard and stone. It would take forever to finish. After the long days in Baba's small welding shop, my father's and Najib's clothes always ended up with yellowish white sweat stains and black marks from burns or ash.

Zeynab came out of the cramped room that served as a little stable. "At least you don't have to milk and clean up after Torran. I swear that cow hates me. Or she's just mad that Khalid gave her a boy's name." She slung a fresh load of dung from her red plastic bucket onto the wall to fill the crack. Seeing me struggling with Habib, she smiled. "Though I think now maybe you have the more difficult job." She went back into the stable.

Habib bent down out of my reach. "Come on, Habib. I have too much work to do for you to be naughty." He giggled when I straightened him upright and scrubbed his belly, so of course I scrubbed more. "What's so funny, Habib? Is that a camel licking your tummy?"

Habib laughed and blew out, buzzing his lips. Steel clattered behind me, and I turned to see Khalid on his bottom next to the piece of metal.

"See?" I shrugged. "I told you not to climb that thing."

"I want to see the Americans!" Khalid got up and dusted himself off. "It's not fair. You got to see them. I want to see them!"

"Khalid, they're soldiers. You don't want anything to do with them. You could get hurt." I picked up Habib and dried him off.

"Then why did Baba and Najib go out to see them?"

"Because they are a lot bigger than you."

"Zu-lay-kah…" Khalid drew out my name in a long whine.

"No, Khalid," I said. When Habib was dry, I slipped a big clean shirt on him and let him pull up his pants, helping him tie the drawstring. "You're next in the bath. And get out of those clothes. I need to wash them too."

Khalid clenched his fists tightly at his sides, his lips pursed in a little *o*. "You always tell me what to do."

"Khalid, you must understand—"

"You think you're so special just because you're older, but you're not. You're just a stupid donkey-faced girl." He spun round and darted off around the side of our house toward the front courtyard. I took a step back, gripping my mouth tight with my hand so that my teeth dug into my fingers.

"Khalid," I whispered.

Habib turned toward me with a sad look on his face. I forced myself to smile at him. Then he was off to play, leaving me as quickly as Khalid had.

The sun hung straight above us now and the heat filled the air, blasting my wet face like a fire. Always before, the ugly words had been outside the walls. Now they were inside too, inside my family's private world...

Before, Khalid had always spoken with a small, sweet voice, but now he sounded as angry and hurtful as Anwar.

3

Hours later, my hands, especially my knuckles, were raw from scrubbing. My neck ached between my shoulders, and my back hurt when I bowed for the midday prayer. I wrung out another of Najib's threadbare shirts and hung it on the line. During the rainless summer, the clothes would dry very quickly. In fact, the first clothes I'd hung up were already dry and crisp, ready to be taken down. But just as I reached for the last shirt, I heard the clang of the metal door slamming in the front courtyard.

"Allahu Akbar!" Baba shouted almost as loud as the morning call to prayer.

I forgot about the clothes and ran into the house through the back door. Zeynab put down the embroidery she was doing on her wedding dress, which she and I always worked on for whenever she would get married. Habib tottered into the room, running as fast as his short stubby legs could carry him. I swept him up. "Ah! Got you, bacha!"

He giggled and kicked his feet until I gently put him down.

Baba and Najib burst into the main room of the house.

"What is it, Baba-jan?" Zeynab asked.

"Everyone! I have good news. Najibullah and I are going to make a lot of money! Hajji Abdullah has just won the bid on another contract right here in An Daral, and he wants Najibullah and me— No. Wait." He looked at Najib. "He wants Frouton Welding Company of An Daral to do all the metalwork. The Americans ordered a school built for Afghan children, and Hajji Abdullah needs us to supervise the project while he is away in Farah."

"Baba!" Zeynab jumped up from the floor. He rushed to her, wrapping his big arm around her. "Baba, I'm all stinky from Torran!" She giggled.

It looked like Baba had his hands full with Zeynab, so I stayed back, but he laughed and held his other arm out to me. "Come here, my beautiful girl." I went to him and smiled, leaning my head against him when he pulled us closer. He kissed both of us on our heads in turn. Despite my mouth, he always made sure that he showed how much he loved all of us. I loved him even more for that. "Here, girls."

He reached into his pocket and pulled out shiny new hair clips, two for each of us. I slipped mine in my pocket, but Zeynab put hers in right away.

"Tashakor, Baba-jan." Zeynab leaned forward and kissed our father's cheek. I wished I could have kissed him, but my lips weren't made for it.

Najib took a few steps back to the corner. "Good for you, Najib," I said to him as Baba let Zeynab and me go. Najib only shrugged with a little smile. Habib ran straight to Baba and threw his arms around Baba's leg.

"Where—" Malehkah started.

"But that's not all!" Baba's voice roared like a deep cannon. He held his hands up, spread wide as if his news were so big he could hardly support it all. "With the money from the school project here in An Daral, Najibullah and I will be able to buy a car." His eyes were alive with an excitement I had not seen in him since before Madar-jan died.

"Not a new car," Najib explained.

"No." Baba shrugged. "Not a new car from the factory. But a good steady one." He punched his fist forward at the word *steady*. "And we'll need it too, to get back and forth from Farah."

"Farah?" Malehkah was sitting, cleaning a chicken

on a board on the floor. "Where is—"

"This is the best part! Our good friend Hajji Abdullah was the one in charge of building the base for the American soldiers in Farah. He did a fine job too. I've seen his photographs. But those rich Americans, they say the buildings are too small! They need more housing for the soldiers to sleep in. They need a new building for their television. Hajji says it's as big as a movie screen!"

"A movie screen," said Zeynab. "I've never seen a movie screen."

Malehkah frowned at her and shook her head.

"I have," Baba replied. "Once when I was a young boy. Back home in Kabul. But that was a different time." He looked down to the floor, then out the front window into the courtyard. "A different Afghanistan. Before the Russians and the wars and then the Taliban."

I wished Zeynab hadn't said anything. Somehow it had made Baba-jan sad. The only noise was the squishing of the chicken as Malehkah prepared it. Habib wandered over toward Malehkah, reaching for some of the chicken parts. I picked him up and bounced him on my hip.

"Hajji Abdullah says the Americans make him

29

hire local men to work on projects," said Najib. "But his welder in Farah is no good. All his welds are coming apart."

"That's because that welder in Farah is a no-good jackal from Pakistan." Baba waved his hand as if to brush away the idea of the Pakistani. "So this is really the best part. In a few months, we'll be making a lot of money working in Farah as well!"

Najib spoke up. "The Americans need the best welders for their big base!"

"Wah wah, Najib!" Zeynab squealed.

Baba slapped Najib on the back. He had to reach up now that Najib had grown taller. "Who knows, but I may even take another wife! I'm not young. This is true. But today I feel as though I am only nineteen, like Najibullah."

Another wife? I shifted my weight onto my other foot. Was he serious? I looked to Zeynab, who stared back and wrinkled her nose at me. Malehkah just chopped at the chicken, saying nothing. But when she looked up, her wide eyes met mine for an instant before she quickly turned away.

"Maybe we'll even make enough money to buy a *big* truck, a welding truck with all our gear on the back." Baba-jan made a frame with his fingers.

"And 'Frouton Welding Company' written on the side in Dari *and* English!"

Malehkah slapped her knife down on the cutting board. "Where's Khalid?"

"What?" Baba's face took on the faint hint of a scowl. He hadn't been listening, so lost was he in his happy dream.

"Where is Khalid?" Malehkah stared at me.

"Not in the back courtyard," I said. My whole body began to slump with the bad feeling I was getting. Why hadn't I been watching him more closely?

Zeynab looked at Malehkah and then at me. "I haven't seen him in the house, but maybe—"

"That's why the street door was unlocked. He must have gone out to see the soldiers," said Baba.

"Zulaikha, I told you to watch the boys," Malehkah said.

"I *told* him he couldn't go."

"Bah. Let him play." Baba backhanded our concerns out of his way with the same movement he used to shoo flies from his rice. He reached into his pocket again and pulled out a shiny caramel, unwrapping it for Habib. "Here, bacha. You eat this. I'll give Khalid his when he gets home."

"But Sadiq, Khalid is just—"

"I said let him play!" Baba shouted. He slapped the wall, then paced to the front window in the silence. When he turned around, he spoke very quietly. "I'll not be contradicted in my own house." He glared at Malehkah. "Khalid is a growing boy. He is getting too old to listen to women."

My mouth hung open at Baba's words. I watched Malehkah take in a breath to speak, then press her lips together to let it out through her nose. She couldn't argue with Baba, but her anger was clear, and Malehkah had ways of forcing me to regret her anger.

Najib had taken a seat on the floor and Baba lay down on the other side of the room. His eyes were heavy and he spread his arms and legs to try to keep cool.

"Hot," said Baba. He reached for Habib when he saw the little one blinking sleepily. "We'll sleep off the hot day, bacha. Nobody can weld in this heat." He kissed Habib on top of his head as the boy settled down. He turned to Najib. "We'll work this evening and maybe late tonight."

Malehkah took the chicken into the tiny kitchen in the back of the house. Zeynab sat down on a rolled-up toshak and resumed sewing. Only the tiny pop of her needle pierced the quiet. Nobody made a sound, and the thick, hot, dusty air was completely still. After a few minutes, Baba's voice, smoother, slower, and quieter than before, interrupted the silence. "Bale. Good times ahead."

For the rest of the afternoon, we would have to do only the quiet chores. Any work like scrubbing the morning's dirty pot or sweeping would have to wait until after the men were awake again.

I went outside to gather the clothes. I always liked the way the dry clothes would try to hold their shape when they came off the line. Draping the clean laundry over my shoulder, I turned back toward the house.

Zeynab tiptoed out and joined me. "I wanted to know if you needed help, but it looks like you have it all taken care of."

"That's okay."

"Isn't it wonderful, Zulaikha? With Baba and Najib and everything?" she whispered. She spun around with her arms outstretched. "I feel like anything is possible."

"What do you mean?" I covered my smile. Zeynab's happiness was always contagious.

"You saw how happy Baba was? My some-day

33

husband will be that joyful when he comes home, just because he'll be glad to see me." Zeynab spun me around like we were dancing. "My husband will know everything about me, and he'll love me even more for it." She squeezed me. "He and I will have maybe three boys and three beautiful girls and he'll be rich enough to hire servants so our kids won't have to do all this cleaning."

I sighed. "It sounds perfect."

"Anyway, aren't you going to tell me what they were like?"

"The Americans?"

"Of course! I hear they are very handsome." She leaned close to me. "Maybe next time they are in town I will go out to see them. One good thing about the chadri is they'd never know I was looking at them."

I slapped her with the clothes and we giggled, our faces close together. Sometimes, I could hardly believe this girl was my sister. She could be so naughty. "The chadri is supposed to prevent strange men from looking at you," I said, reaching around with my free hand to tickle her side. She jumped and pushed me away. "Not to help you make sexy eyes at dangerous soldiers."

Zeynab laughed. "Maybe I like dangerous—"

She stopped. I turned to see what she was looking at. Malehkah stood with her hands on her hips, leaning back to support the weight of her unborn baby. I didn't know how long she'd been there. "What's dangerous is you talking dirty and risking a bad reputation," she said. "You'll make it impossible for your father to find you a husband. Don't think it's that far away."

"Oh, I *know*, Madar." Zeynab beamed. She squeezed my hand. I squeezed back. "We were just talking about how great it will be when Baba and Najib get their wonderful new jobs."

Malehkah stared at Zeynab. "Zulaikha." She spoke my name like a curse word. "Go to the bazaar. We need rice. Get also a couple of oranges or a few bananas if you can find any that aren't too rotten."

"I can go to the bazaar for you," Zeynab offered.

Malehkah smiled, but not kindly. "Tashakor, Zeynab, but it is not good for an attractive young unmarried woman to be running about town on her own. Zulaikha can go."

I squeezed my sister's hand again and gave her the clean clothes. I wasn't stupid. Malehkah had plenty of rice and I knew the oranges and bananas weren't meant for our meal tonight. I reached for

35

the small roll of Afghanis in her hand, but she just looked down at me, forcing a smile that made small wrinkles around her eyes.

"Stay away from the soldiers, Zulaikha. They cannot be trusted. And while you are out, if you see Khalid, will you ask him to come home?"

She phrased it as a question, but it was most certainly not a request.

"Bale, Madar," I said quietly. And for the second time that day, I left our compound.

4

An Daral was a large village, full of winding streets lined with walls of stacked rocks or mud-brick. With so many walls, I had to always be walking around a compound or a garden to look for Khalid. The soccer field was an empty stretch of packed dust. Little whirlwinds of sand were all that played there. He was not swimming in any of the three popular deep spots in the river, though the crushing heat made me envious of those who were. And even though finding the Americans might have helped me find my brother, I was glad when there wasn't a single soldier anywhere.

By the time I reached the bazaar, several shop owners were lowering their shutters to close up until it cooled off a little. I was lucky to have made it before everything was closed. I couldn't wait until evening for the shops to open again. By that time, Khalid would have gone home on his own, if he wasn't there already, having a good laugh about making me run all over town in this heat.

I haggled forever with the man selling fruit. He must have thought I was dumb and didn't know how much the other women paid for oranges. By the time I'd argued my way to a fair price, most of the shops were locked up behind their shutters. Carrying my purchases in the small plastic sack from the rice man, I set off for the last place I might find Khalid.

Part of me hoped I would not find him there.

I had to go through the butcher district. The bees and flies buzzed all about the cuts of beef and mutton that had swung from hooks since this morning's slaughter. The blood that stained the ground cooked in the glare of the sun and let off a sour-sweet stench that stung my eyes and nose. At the end of the street, I stepped out into the empty space that surrounded the Citadel.

The Citadel loomed twice as tall as the tallest building in An Daral – a colossal mudstone castle that had baked under the Afghan sun since before time. It might have been home to kings once, but it now housed only old Russian war junk. Provincial police supposedly kept watch to make sure people stayed away, but they must not have tried very hard, because kids often played in, around, and on top of the walls of the giant fortress.

Being a girl, I had never been to the Citadel, but years ago Najib had gone to play there and he'd told Zeynab and me all about it. When Baba found out, he beat Najib's bottom. If the old Russian guns and bombs that were left there from the war weren't dangerous enough, Baba said there were cracks in the walls and plenty of steep places to fall from.

It would have taken a very long time to circle the whole Citadel. I was grateful, then, when I found Khalid quickly. I was not so happy with where he was. Or who he was with.

He was crouched on a large mudstone boulder fifteen or twenty meters up one of the giant fissures in the ancient wall. Anwar and his cousins stood under a date tree at the bottom of the wall, looking up at him. "Come on, you little baby," Anwar shouted. "It's an easy climb. If you want to play with us, you need to make it all the way to the top."

I was not surprised to see Anwar involved in this. Why couldn't he just leave people alone? I slid down to hide in the bottom of a dried-out irrigation ditch where I could watch the boys without being seen. Khalid was high above us all and he wasn't even to the top of the wall yet. My legs shook and my hands sweated as I watched him. But what could I do with Anwar and his cousins out there?

"What are you waiting for?" Anwar shouted. He picked up a rock and threw it at my brother. It struck the wall over a meter below Khalid, who turned and looked down. His face looked pale against the darker mudstone. His bottom lip quivered and he wiped his eyes. Anwar picked up another rock. "Oh, little baby going to cry?" He laughed. "You're as scared as Donkeyface!"

"I am not!" Khalid turned back to the wall and reached a shaky little hand for a hold above him, making his way up again. "I just… "

Omar threw a rock so that it hit the wall even closer to Khalid. "Keep climbing, baby. Hurry up."

"Please." Khalid began to sob. "Please… stop it."

Salman and Anwar threw more rocks. One hit Khalid in the leg. He jerked so much that I feared he would fall.

For a moment, I thought maybe Khalid deserved what he was getting. His cruel words had hurt me worse than anything Anwar had ever done. But when I saw the tears rolling down his cheeks, I remembered how I had fed, cleaned, and comforted him when he was a baby. Whatever he had done, he was still my brother, and I couldn't let him get hurt over some stupid dare. I put down my sack of food and tied my chador on tight. Then I gripped a tree root and climbed up out of my hiding place. I ran to the wall as fast as I could. "Khalid, come down from there!"

Anwar and his cousins whooped when they saw me. "Oh, look who's come to save the little baby! Well, go on, Donkeyface. See if you can climb up there and rescue your stupid brother."

I scrambled up a steep path within the crevasse. Then I found a handhold and a small ledge. I had to pull my skirt up unthinkably high, almost to my knees, in order to climb up to the next small landing where I could look for another path.

Khalid turned and looked down. He wiped the tears from his eyes. "Zulaikha, what are you doing? Go away!"

"He's going to give up! Just because of his ugly sister." Omar laughed.

Anwar had stopped paying attention to Khalid. "Put your skirt down, dirty girl!"

As much as I hated him, Anwar was right. Good Afghan girls did not climb. But I blew a strand of hair out of my face and kept going after Khalid. Maybe proper Afghan girls were not to be seen climbing with their skirts to their knees, but since birth, I had never looked like a proper Afghan girl.

I moved quickly, sometimes scaling straight up, sometimes finding a path that would take me a few meters. Soon I made it up to where Khalid was stuck.

"Come on," I said. "There's a place to hold on to just above you." I leaned against the mudstone and begged Allah to keep me from falling. Then I slid my leg out along the small outcropping where we both stood. "We're almost to the top. Step on my leg and boost yourself up to the next ledge." I put my hand on Khalid's back. "I'll hold you to the wall. Come on. You can do it. We can't go back the way we came. Not with those boys down there."

Slowly he put his foot on my thigh. I did my best to press him to the wall as he climbed. When he was on the ledge, he found another path and scaled some small boulders until he finally reached the top of the Citadel. He stood and pumped his arms in the air, strutting around like he'd just won a big race or something. "You can see far from up here!" he shouted.

I sighed with relief. Khalid had made it to the top without falling. For the moment, he was a little safer, but there were still plenty of ways for him to be hurt. Now I just had to get there myself, then find a safe way back down.

Finally, I came up out of the fissure into the hot, bright sun. I blinked in the glare and marveled for one moment at the sheer enormity of the fortress. High walls, more like mountains, ringed a scrub grass field far below, which was speckled with Russian junk and more ruins. The entire castle covered a square kilometer at least. When I looked back toward town, I was relieved to see that Anwar and his gang had gone. I could hardly believe my brother thought it worthwhile to risk both our lives for a monster who ran away and forgot about him.

Now where was Khalid?

The wind blew against my face. Its heat felt good whipping through my sweat-damp hair. My brother stood on a narrow strip of ancient mudstone no wider than the length of my arm. It was a sort of land bridge to the next enormous tower, huge sections of the wall having collapsed long ago. He was shaking with fear and looking down to the ground far below. "I… I can't move, Zulaikha."

"Khalid, just calm down. I'll help you." But I had no idea what to do. The thin mudstone bridge wasn't really big enough for both of us. I'd fall, or I'd scare Khalid and he'd fall, taking me with him. My legs shook as I took small steps toward the land bridge, reaching out my hand. "Come on, Khalid. Come to me. Take my hand."

"Stop right there!" a man shouted.

Khalid jumped at the unexpected voice. He wheeled his arms to keep his balance before crouching down low on the narrow strip of wall. His eyes welled up with fearful tears. As soon as I knew he wasn't falling, I turned to see a policeman three towers away, rifle in hand, coming toward us fast.

So that was why Anwar and the boys had fled. They must have seen the policeman coming and run away, leaving Khalid and me in trouble.

"Khalid," I said. "You've got to run! Run or you'll be caught!"

"I can't," he cried, shaking his head. "I'm stuck! Help me."

"You two, get over here!" The policeman shook his rifle in the air.

I clenched a fist. Slowly, I made my way out onto the tiny strip of mudstone. Walking sideways, I slid my right foot forward, and then trailed my left foot behind it. Bit by bit, I made my way closer and closer to Khalid.

At home, Zeynab was always nervous whenever she was near the edge of the roof of our house. I had never had any such fears. But now my palms were sweaty and my knees shook as I looked straight down. Below me was empty space all the way to the hard ground, where a shepherd boy and his little grazing flock looked like small white dots. A wind gusted against my back.

"We're going to fall," Khalid whispered.

"No, we're not," I managed to whisper back. Then I realized I'd barely made a sound. "We're not going to fall," I repeated, louder. The policeman clambered toward us along the uneven top of the wall. "Khalid, we have to go. If we don't, we'll be arrested."

"I can't. I can't move, Zulaikha. I can't."

I pulled my bottom lip up tight over my teeth, took a deep breath, and with a prayer to Allah, ran several quick steps to my brother. Another gust of wind tried to push me off the wall as I bent down. "Khalid, there is no difference between where you're standing and the front courtyard back home. This is just higher up. Now you will stand up *right now* or I'll pull you up."

He just crouched there, shaking his head and crying. But when I reached for him, he stood up on his own shaky legs. Then he took a step backward. Half of his foot landed on an uneven rock. Off-balance and terrified, he scrambled to get sure footing.

"Khalid, stop!"

His right foot stepped sideways and slipped off the edge. He flailed his arms back, shrieking. I bolted forward, hooked my arms under his, and pulled his little body up as I ran across the mudstone bridge. I threw us both down on the flat top of the next tower.

"You kids come back here!" The policeman was only two towers away and running now. Khalid's eyes were wide and his breathing fast. He looked at the policeman and then at me.

"Come on. We have to go," I said.

We got up and ran along the top of the wall, looking for a way down. Suddenly, Khalid stopped and pointed to another large crevasse in the wall. "Here. Climb down."

"You first," I said.

Khalid lay down on his belly and slipped down to the little pathway below. I didn't waste any time, but hurried after him. Just before my head ducked below the top, I saw the policeman making his way across the narrow strip of wall. My hands shook. Climbing down was more difficult than climbing up.

I couldn't always see what was below me.

"Stop!" The man's voice came from above. He was very close now. I tried to move faster, but my dress kept catching on clumps of mudstone. I pulled my skirt up a little and kept going.

"Hurry!" Khalid had reached the ground. He jumped up and down. "Hurry, Zulaikha!"

"Just go. I'll catch up. Run!" When he still waited for me, I shouted again. "Go home! Get out of here!"

Wiping tears from his eyes, Khalid ran off faster than I've ever seen him run before. I brushed the sweat from my brow. *Thanks and praise be to Allah the most merciful. Thank you for saving my brother.*

A few pebbles rolled down the steep face of the wall from above. Khalid was safe, but I was not. The policeman was climbing down. If I ever got out of jail, my father would beat me until I was raw. *Oh, Allah, be merciful. Please help me.*

My hand slipped loose. I skidded down a steep incline, righting myself on a small ledge. But I was moving too fast to get control. The rest of my descent to the ground was a series of slides, scrapes, and rolls. When I reached the gentler slope at the base of the wall, I didn't even take the time to look back. I got to my feet and ran across the dusty clearing toward the nearest houses. Just ahead was the irrigation ditch. Climbing down to the bottom and back up the other side would take too long. The policeman would be on me by then. This section of the ditch was only maybe a meter wide. I pulled my skirt up just a little higher and sped up, snapping each leg down as fast as I could. I reached the trench and jumped.

Only when my feet hit the ground on the other side did I risk a look back. The policeman was still after me, and he meant to jump the trench too. My legs hurt. I wanted to stop. I knew I couldn't outrun this man. I rounded a corner of one of the walls at the edge of the Citadel yards and cleared the first compound.

Then a hand was on my arm. It pulled me around hard, and I gasped. How had the policeman closed the gap so quickly? I crashed into the wall next to me and struggled to hold on to my filthy chador.

"Come with me, child." It was an old woman. She pulled me back away from the street into a narrow walkway between two walls. Then she dragged a rusted piece of sheet metal over the entry, tying it in place with several old ropes fixed to rusted steel bolts in the mudstone.

"Who—"

She turned and faced me, holding a finger to her lips. I opened my mouth wide so that my heavy breathing didn't whistle through my teeth. From the other side of the makeshift scrap-metal door came the sound of heavy boots. They stopped right outside. I was trapped! I spun around, looking for another way out, but the woman put a hand on my shoulder and gently turned me back toward her. I jerked my shoulder to get away. She held her hands back from me and smiled, nodding as if to tell me that I was safe with her. We both stood very still.

It seemed like we waited for a very long time.

From out in the street came a quiet *pop* and a hissing sound. A moment later, I could smell cigarette smoke. There was a cough and then the sound of footsteps moving away.

When a minute or two had passed, the woman said, "There. He's gone." She looked me over and then reached out to pat my shoulder. "You're still shaking. You've had quite a scare, rushing down the Citadel wall like that. Come with me. We'll have a cup of tea and you can take some time to relax and collect yourself." She squeezed by me in the narrow passage. When I didn't follow her, she smiled "Really, child. Come along. You can't go out there right now anyway. He may still be looking for you."

There was something strangely comforting in her smile and in the sound of her voice. Maybe I could trust her, at least enough to have a simple cup of tea.

5

I sat on a plastic chair and looked around the tiny apartment. The walls were decorated with a few small postcards, pictures of mosques and of the old statues at Bamiyan. The woman turned from her cook plate and handed me a cup of tea. She sat down on the bed. That and the small bedside table were the only other pieces of furniture in the room.

She did not speak for a while, cradling her cup and taking time to let the tea cool. On the small table next to her was a faded photograph in a cracked frame. It was of an older man with flecks of gray in his hair, but in his eyes was a look of confidence and kindness. She followed my gaze. "My husband." She gently ran her fingers over the picture. "Masoud was a great man. I miss him very much." I didn't know what to say. Maybe she didn't either, because it was quiet for a moment. "What do you think? My little sewing shop is on the other side of the curtain. More and more business lately. Some of the chadris are finally coming off and lots of women need old dresses fixed up. It seems that I spend most of my time over there." She shrugged. "I suppose that's progress."

I took a sip of my tea, putting my head back so I wouldn't dribble, and I felt the warmth calm through my body. "Tashakor," I said, "for helping me get away."

"It was the least I could do for a girl brave enough to go all the way up there to rescue her little brother." She must have noticed my scowl at the mention of Khalid. "Getting to that age, is he? Wants to be the big man who doesn't have to listen to anyone?"

How did she know? "It seems that in one day he has decided to hate me. He called me... bad names."

The woman took another sip of tea. "Give the boy time, child. He'll need help with something one day, or he'll want some sweet cake you've made, and he'll be nicer." She laughed. "Who knows, but one day, Zulaikha, he may even thank you for saving his life on the Citadel wall." She nodded at my wide eyes. "Oh, yes, child. Doubtless you do not remember me, but I certainly remember you. And your mother."

"My mother—"

"Was a great woman. Such a love for books. And for poetry."

What was she talking about? Did this old lady have me confused with someone else? But she knew my name. "I don't... I mean... Who are you?"

"My name is Meena. Years ago, before the wars, before the Russians came, I was a professor of literature at the university in Herat."

I had to put the cup down before I dropped it. "My mother went to Herat?"

"No, child." She spoke so softly that I had to lean forward to hear. "When the Russians leveled Herat, I fled to An Daral with my husband." She took a deep breath. "And we were so happy for a while. Masoud was wonderful. He loved me. He loved my work. But the wars took him too." She did not speak for a moment, and the silence in the room felt heavy. "But even then, I was not alone. I found a group of men and women who loved literature and the ancient Afghan poets as much as I did. In the dark days when the Taliban ruled everything, we met in secret. Without my fellow book lovers, I would have lost the last threads of my hope."

"I remember," I said slowly. "Strangers in the house, all drinking tea and reading passages from books. Talking about things and laughing." I shook my head. "I never understood who they were.

I thought they were relatives visiting from Kabul."

"In many ways we were like a family. We were very close until the Taliban found out about our meetings."

I was grateful when she didn't go on. I didn't like to think about the Taliban.

She sighed. "Ah, Zulaikha, the beautiful princess. How you've grown."

"I'm only a girl." I covered my mouth with my filthy chador. "I'm not beautiful."

"Only a girl?" She reached toward me and gently pulled the shawl away from my face. "Nonsense. There's nothing 'only' about being a girl. You must give yourself time. 'Every triumph from patience springs, the happy herald of better things.'"

I had always thought those words were something my mother shared only with me. How could Meena know them? "That's what my mother used to say."

"Yes." She smiled. "I know. It comes from *Yusuf and Zulaikha*. Your mother adored the poet Jami. And you. So you will forgive me, Zulaikha-jan, if I cannot accept that you are, as you say, 'only a girl'."

"She tried to teach me to read, but I can only remember a few words. Letters," I said. I stared down into my cup. When I could have asked so many important questions about my mother, all I could do was say something dumb.

Meena leaned forward so the light from the one tiny window showed her face. Though she looked old, her eyes glimmered with excitement. "Ah, Zulaikha. Long ago, in Herat…" She stopped for so long that I thought she'd finished. But finally she went on. "Long ago in Herat, I taught literature and poetry. The best our ancient culture had to offer. My students would greet me as they came into class, boys and girls both. 'Salaam alaikum, Muallem-sahib.'" Her breath sounded shaky, like the plastic sheet that fluttered in one of our windows. "You've never heard about poets like Firdawsi, Jami, Hafez, or Abdullah Ansari, whose tomb in Herat rivals even its Great Mosque in beauty. You've never heard of *Yusuf and Zulaikha*, even though it was your mother's favorite poem. No. No, of course you haven't. You know only war." Her voice trailed off to a whisper. "In all of Afghanistan… only war."

She closed her eyes and leaned her head back. Somehow, even though she was still right in front of me, she looked as if she had traveled far away.

"You see, Zulaikha-jan, we've lost so much. But if we lose our literature, our poetry," she said, "not only

Afghanistan, but the whole world will suffer."

I was going to say something but she was already speaking.

> *"His daughter Zulaikha's loveliness*
> *Made her look like a true princess.*
> *The brightest star set in his night,*
> *The richest jewel held by his sight.*
> *What poem could capture her beauty? None..."*

She rocked back and forth as she spoke, her last words trailing off in whispers as a wind moaned through the room. The sound, the rhythm, the tone of her voice wrapped around me. Even when her words had faded away, she kept rocking silently.

I wanted her to continue. There was something about the words that drew me in. As she recited, I remembered the brilliant silver arc of the crescent moon. The whisper of wind in the leaves of our date tree. The warm, safe walls of home. Most of all, her words reminded me of my mother.

"How can you remember all of that?" I whispered.

"Tsh, tsh, tsh." She waved a crooked finger. "Your mother could recite far more. She wanted to memorize the entire book so that the Taliban could never steal the poetry from her."

A low ache started in my stomach and spread to my chest. I wiped my eyes as I fought those bad memories. "But they did—"

"They did nothing!" She straightened up so fast that a splash of tea spilled over the side of her cup, splattering on the floor. "They tried to ban everything besides the Holy Quran, anything that didn't fit with their twisted idea of Islam. But Afghanistan's literature has survived thousands of years and a half dozen armies far more powerful than the Taliban's wretched rabble."

I looked at Meena, this old woman with kind eyes, nearly white hair, and skin as wrinkled as a ripe pomegranate. "Madar-jan tried to teach me. I promised her I would learn all I could. I try to remember but…" I had so little to remember my mother by. And suddenly, as if by Allah's miracle, I knew what I needed to do. "I want to learn to read and to write. I want to know about the poems my mother loved," I said. "Will you teach me?"

"Child," said Meena with a smile. "It would be my honor."

"Where have you been?" Malehkah's voice was low as I stepped into the compound.

"Madar." I made an attempt to brush some of the sand and dirt from my dress and chador. "I was looking for Khalid."

She stepped very close, pinning me against the wall. "Khalid is *here*!" I could feel her breath on my face as she spoke. "He told me where you were."

Oh, no. What would Baba do if Malehkah told him I'd had tea with Meena? But how could Khalid have known where I was? He'd been far ahead of me when we ran.

"The Citadel!" she spat through clenched teeth.

I never thought I would be almost relieved to be scolded about the fortress.

"He was stuck."

"You blame this on Khalid?" She stood up straight and snatched the bag of food that I'd recovered from the dry irrigation ditch after leaving Meena's house.

"I tried to help him, Malehkah. I ran after—"

She grabbed my shoulders and pushed me up against the wall. "While you live in this house, you will show me proper respect and call me 'Mother'."

She gave me another shove and stepped away from me. "Khalid told me how you chased after him. How you chased him up to the top of the wall where he almost fell."

"I didn't—"

"Running all over town and climbing like a man. Keep acting like this and no man will ever want you, even if we could find someone willing to overlook your mouth. We'll never marry you off. You disgust me." She turned away and marched back toward the house.

"But he..." I stammered. "I saved—"

"Help your sister sort rice. She's on the back porch." Malehkah vanished into the house.

I could have died trying to save that little jackal, and now I was in trouble for what he had done. I held my fist to my mouth until my teeth dug into my hand.

"Zulaikha!" Malehkah leaned out the window. "Go help your sister. Stop standing around sniveling."

"Bale... Madar." I stepped into the house.

On the back porch, I helped Zeynab pick the bad bits and the bugs out of the rice. We worked in silence for a few minutes.

"I've already spoken to her about it," Zeynab

whispered. She squeezed my hand. "Don't worry. She said she's not going to tell Baba about the Citadel. She doesn't want to risk her precious Khalid getting a beating."

For a moment I thought about telling my sister about my new muallem. Zeynab and I told each other everything. But there was something about the mystery of the woman and the excitement of beginning my studies... It was my discovery, and I wasn't willing to share it yet.

"What is it?" Zeynab was watching me.

"Nothing," I said. But she kept looking at me. "Really," I said.

I went back to picking the ugly bits out of the rice.

✷ ✷ ✷

That night after the evening prayer, I watched from the roof as Baba and Najib prepared themselves for a long night of welding.

"I think there is space in the back corner of the compound, Najibullah, for a little storage room to keep all the new equipment we're going to need. Maybe we could build it with cement blocks instead of mud brick." Baba-jan smiled and held up his hands as though he could touch the cement. His words and laughter echoed off the walls in the front courtyard, cutting through the stillness of the blue time at the day's end. "Huh, Najibullah? Just like the Americans use for the walls of their base. Nothing is too good for us."

They left the compound, and Malehkah closed and locked the door behind them. But even with the door closed, I could still hear Baba's voice as he and my older brother walked away. Poor Najib. He was Baba's oldest son, my father's favorite by far, and yet he hardly had the chance to speak around my energetic baba.

Over the mountain to the east shone the bright edge of the rising crescent moon. With a sigh, I lay back against the dome of our house, watching the moonrise. Today had been the most unusual day I could remember. It started with Malehkah angry with me. It ended with Malehkah furious with me. And in between I had experienced almost every emotion I could think of. I clenched my fists with the memory of Anwar's cruel words and of Khalid repeating them.

Though I'd seen the moon countless times before, somehow tonight it smiled on something new.

It wasn't just my father's hopes for a great fortune from working with the Americans. As my eyelids became heavy and my breathing steadied and deepened, I remembered the feeling of ancient power and wisdom in Meena's words. I thought about her promise to teach me, and about the slow, rhythmic sounds of the old muallem's poetry.

6

All of my efforts to get back to Meena throughout the next week failed. The best I could do was work on my letters. Before I left her apartment, Meena had written the Dari alphabet on a little scrap of paper I carried in my pocket. When I could find time by myself, I practiced writing the letters in the dust, connecting each one with the sound it made. Madar-jan had taught me most of this years ago, and so I was happy to find that I quickly improved. Still, I needed more time for writing. If only I didn't have so many chores.

Water sloshed from my heavy bucket as I sidestepped my younger brothers in the garden. "Boys," I said. "Can you get out of the way?" Habib picked up his little plastic soldiers and moved aside. Khalid didn't. Even though I'd saved him at the Citadel only a week ago, he still seemed to take new pleasure in being a "growing boy".

"Khalid, won't you step aside a little and let your

sisters water the plants?" Zeynab smiled at him as she carried the second bucket.

He picked up his toys and went to the other end of the garden. Of course. I should have known. Khalid still listened to girls. He just didn't listen to me. I refused to show how much it bothered me. "Tashakor, Zeynab," I said. I poured water into a shallow irrigation trench for the thirsty eggplants, onions, and carrots.

Zeynab shrugged. "You see? It's all in the way you talk to the little bacha."

We went back to the well. I pulled the rope to bring up the pail. In summer, the garden had to be watered heavily once in the morning and again at night. It was a long process each time.

"Habib, bring your men up on this hill. That can be your base." Khalid pointed to a small depression in the dirt, around which he'd piled up a wall a few centimeters high. His own plastic soldiers were exactly like Habib's green ones, except Khalid's were tan. Tan – just like the uniforms of the American soldiers, he said.

Habib looked at me for a moment as if to check if it was okay, then tottered around the pomegranate bush to join Khalid. I poured water into Zeynab's bucket and then dropped the empty pail back down the deep well.

Zeynab smiled and motioned for me to be quiet. She watched the boys. Maybe she was dreaming again of her own future sons. She was always talking about how cute they would be. I hoped that any children she might someday have would be cuter than Khalid. For days now, ever since Najib and Baba had returned from Herat with a handful of toy soldiers and the new white Toyota, the armies of Khalid and Habib had been having endless battles.

"Shrooooom!" Khalid spat as he made one of his men shoot, tracing a line with his finger toward Habib's base. "Rocket launcher. Quick, Habib, get your men out of the way."

As Habib watched, Khalid stepped over and knocked down three of his little brother's soldiers. "Too late. Heat-seeking rockets. Can't dodge them."

Khalid let Habib shoot down one of his men. Habib wanted two, but Khalid claimed the second was not hurt thanks to special armor. Then, as always, the more powerful weapons of the great American army killed all of Habib's green Pakistani men. Habib frowned and started to walk away, leaving his men lying dead in the dirt.

"Where are you going? Let's play again!" Khalid tugged gently on the sleeve of Habib's perahan-tunban to keep him from getting away. Habib twisted out of his grip and went for the house.

"Maybe you should have had your Americans build him a school," I said.

Khalid scowled at me and went after his brother. I hated that mean look of his. Meena had said this angry phase would pass. I hoped she was right.

"Zulaikha?"

I turned away from my brothers.

"Are you okay?" Zeynab said.

"Sure," I said. "I'm fine. Just thinking."

"About what?"

I could not tell her about Meena. If I told her now, she would be hurt that I'd kept a secret from her, never mind the fact that it was my first one. "Oh, about Herat, and Baba's new car, I guess."

"Oh, yes. That wonderful car." Zeynab pulled hand over hand on the rope to bring another pail of water up to fill my bucket. "It's great that Baba is doing so well. He was right. These are good times."

"Even if the car is already broken."

Zeynab laughed. "Sure," she said. "But it's not

just the car. That's exciting, yes, but for the first time in years, Baba doesn't have to worry so much about keeping his family fed. He's becoming a respected man. He'll make lots of money with the new construction job."

I frowned. "But you said you didn't like the new school project."

"It *is* all so stupid." Zeynab smacked the pail against the side of the well. "Why does anyone think we need a new school? Just so girls can go? Why don't they work on rebuilding some of the buildings that were wrecked during the wars?"

"If all Baba says is true, they're rebuilding everything up in Herat. Even the old university is open again," I said, wishing I could find a way to tell Meena this news.

My sister took a moment before she shrugged and answered, "This is true." Then her face lit up with her contagious smile. "But who cares about all that? The more important thing, Zulaikha, the most unbelievable part of all of this..." She looked around to make sure nobody was listening. Then she leaned in close. "I heard Baba-jan talking to Najib. He says now that they've got the business with the car taken care of, they can concentrate on arranging the bride-price."

"Have Malehkah and Baba found Najib a wife?"

Zeynab nodded. "They must have. Why else do we have to get everything ready for guests? Baba says it's just business, but I bet he's meeting with someone about a wife for Najib."

"Good." I wiped my brow. "Najib is so nice. He deserves a good wife to start a happy family of his own."

"I just hope she's nicer than Malehkah."

"She must be a good woman," I said. "Baba knows what's best for all of us." I hoped so, for all our sakes. I didn't know what I'd do if another woman like Malehkah came to live with us.

We went to pour water into the cracks in the dirt around the plants.

"I suppose you're right," said Zeynab. "Hey." She touched my arm. "I know what you're thinking." She tipped her water out more carefully than me. She was always more graceful in all she did. "I know that with Najib married, it will be my turn next. But I'm only fifteen. Baba won't be looking to find a match for me for a few years. Look at Najib. He's nineteen. So cheer up. You and I have years left together."

For once Zeynab was wrong – that wasn't what

I had been thinking at all – but I thought about it now as we walked back to the well. Unless Najib's bride liked me, I'd be all alone once Zeynab left. If Najib's wife made friends with Malehkah, I'd have nobody to talk to, except maybe Habib, who hardly talked at all.

"Zulaikha, you're my only sister. Even after I marry we'll visit each other all the time. Then before you know it, you'll have a husband of your own and—"

I tried to smile, but of course my messed-up mouth wouldn't let me. "I'm not beautiful like you. What bride-price would Baba get for me? Maybe one Afghani."

Zeynab let the full pail fall back down into the well, put her arms around me, and squeezed me close. "Zulaikha, that's not true. You have to believe me. I pray for your happiness every day. One day, you'll meet the perfect man who will love you and take care of you. You'll be so happy. Everything will work out."

The boys had settled their dispute and returned to the garden to resume their war. Zeynab and I worked in silence for a few minutes. Why argue with her? Facing a lifetime under Malehkah's rule,

I figured I might as well get used to at least appearing as though I agreed.

"Zulaikha!" It was Malehkah's well-practiced shriek.

"What does she want now?" Zeynab looked to the house.

"Zulaikha! Come here, right now!" Malehkah burst out the back door and motioned for me to follow her. Then she darted back inside.

Zeynab looked at me. Khalid and Habib called a cease-fire from the battle they were about to start.

"Zulaikha! Get in here now or I'm going to beat you!" Malehkah shouted. She was always mean, but she hardly ever hit me.

"Zeynab." My voice and my legs shook.

My sister squeezed my hand. "I'll go with you."

"Hurry up!" Malehkah grabbed my shoulders as soon as I was in the house. She pulled me as close as she could with her big belly and scrubbed at my face with a wet rag. "Khalid!" she called to my little brother, who'd followed us inside. "Take Habib and go help Najibullah fix the car out front."

"Madar, what—"

"Get out there!" Malehkah shouted so loud I jumped. Habib's lower lip began to tremble as it always did before he cried, but Khalid grabbed him by the wrist and pulled him out the front door.

Malehkah wiped at my face until it hurt. I had to pull my lower lip up to cover my upper teeth so they wouldn't snag in the cloth.

Zeynab started, "Madar, can you tell us—"

"Brush her hair." Malehkah thrust a brush into my sister's hand.

Zeynab didn't argue, running Malehkah's hairbrush through my hair. That, at least, was almost comforting. But of course, our father's wife had to ruin everything. "No, no. Not like that." Malehkah snapped the brush from Zeynab's hand. "Go get her Eid dress from her trunk." To me, she added, "You better hope it still fits." Then she cranked the brush through my hair in hard, merciless strokes, yanking out the snarls. If the snarls would not come undone, she simply brushed out whole clumps of hair. It hurt so much that my eyes stung and I couldn't see for the tears.

"Madar, you're hurting me."

"Is she ready yet?" Najib spoke quickly from the front doorway.

"No. Get out, so we can change her clothes,"

said Malehkah. "And you should wash after working on the car."

"No time! I can't get it started." Najib wiped his greasy hands on his perahan-tunban. "We have to walk. Hurry!" He ducked out the door.

"Here." Zeynab held up my pink dress with the lace bottom, which I only wore once a year to celebrate the end of Ramadan.

"Good." Malehkah tugged at my green dress, struggling to pull it off me. "Zulaikha, pull your arms out!" She yanked it off and threw it into a corner. She took hold of the pink dress. "Zeynab, help me put this on her."

"I can dress myself!" I said.

Zeynab brought the pink dress down over my head and I pushed my arms into the sleeves. When my head came out the top and I could see again, Malehkah's face was close to mine, an intense fire in her eyes. "Now you listen to me carefully, Zulaikha. You do exactly as I say." She had a firm grip on my shoulders. "Answer any question they ask you, but don't say anything more. Do whatever they tell you to do. Don't argue. Can you remember that? Your father and Najibullah will try to help you. Be a good girl. Be careful."

She thrust my clean white chador in my hands. Her eyes weren't wrinkled into the squint of her usual scowl. Instead of being grumpy, she sounded worried. Somehow Malehkah was more frightening when she was not angry.

The police from the Citadel. They'd found me somehow. "Madar, what's happening?" I asked.

"Shh," she said, giving my shoulders a squeeze. "Don't cry. You'll make yourself all—"

Najib burst into the room. "Is she ready?" He looked at me, put his arm around my back, and pushed me outside. "Come on. We have to hurry."

"Why, Najib? Where are we going? Where's Baba?"

Najib took me out the front door and all the way to the street. I looked back to see Zeynab and Malehkah watching us go for a moment before they went back inside, closing us out of the compound.

"Najib?" I fought to keep control of my voice. He pulled me along with steps so big I almost had to run to keep up.

He didn't answer right away, but just frowned, stepping around a hole in the road. A boy riding a donkey pulling a cart passed by on the cross street.

"Najib—"

"Baba is down at the work site talking to the Americans," he said quickly. "They've come looking for you."

7

A crowd had gathered near the construction site on the other side of the river. Two large, tan gun-trucks, just like the ones I'd seen that day on the river road, were parked about three car lengths apart with a dusty red pickup between them. American soldiers walked around the trucks wearing helmets and body armor, carrying big rifles. Once again, men stood with their upper bodies out of the top of each truck, manning their guns.

Najib stopped near the worn ruins of a low mudstone wall at the edge of the gathering. He let out a long breath. "Come on."

I wanted to duck down and hide behind the wall. How had the Citadel guards convinced the Americans to come for me so quickly? "I'm scared, Najibullah."

He turned his gaze away from the soldiers and the crowd and really looked at me. His hand reached out and took hold of mine. "Just do what they say. You'll be safe." But he did not sound sure.

What could I do? Baba, Najib, and Malehkah all wanted me to obey the soldiers. Even if I could run away from the army men, I couldn't escape my family. Baba was making a lot of money from their construction projects. He might be angry if I offended the Americans by shaking scared in front of them. He would definitely be angry when he found out about the Citadel.

I tightened my legs and clenched my fists to try to get control, but it did no good. How could I not be scared of these big soldiers and their big guns? Their chests and backs were all boxy. Baba said they wore bulletproof plates to protect themselves. Protect themselves from who? The Taliban were mostly gone. Who else would be foolish enough to try to fight these men? I pulled my shawl up to cover my mouth as Najib gently urged me closer, his hand on my back. "I want to go home. I want to go home. I want to go home," I whispered.

My feet were not my own, so I did not know how I made my way up into the crowd around the Americans. Anwar and his gang lurked at the other end of the circle of people. When I saw them, I shrank back for a moment, but then I saw they were far more interested in the soldiers, asking them for radios

76

and soccer balls. How could they be so free with these men? How were they not afraid?

Maybe because the soldiers weren't hunting them. I looked up at Najib, wishing he would take me home, but he was no help. He led me slowly around a dry rut and toward Baba. Next to him was the African soldier who had noticed my ugly face that day on the river road.

"*Salaam, rafiq!*" the African soldier shouted. He waved at me and turned to some of the other Americans, saying something in English, pointing at me. His right hand was on the handle of the rifle that he kept pointed at the ground. I froze. Najib pushed me forward but my legs were locked.

When the rest of the army men saw me, they smiled and a few rushed toward me. I hid behind my chador. Baba came with them, talking to an Afghan who wore tight, American-style jeans and a gray jacket.

A hand touched my shoulder. I jumped and spun around. Behind me was an American woman wearing the same uniform as the men. She wore the same armor on her chest, the same big helmet, and even the same tan and brown pants, but unlike the other soldiers, her gun was a small pistol at her belt.

I started to step back. Then I remembered what

Malehkah had said, and I stayed where I was. I looked to my family for help. Najib had faded back into the crowd, but Baba moved closer. I hoped he would explain everything to me, but he was silent in the presence of these soldiers.

"*Salaam*," the woman said. She reached up and unsnapped the chin strap of her helmet. When she pulled the helmet off, I could see she had long auburn hair pinned up into a ball on the back of her head with a few long strands loose beside her face. How could she allow herself to be seen completely uncovered in public? What was wrong with her?

She smiled and gently took my hand. Then she said something in English to the man in the gray jacket.

The Afghan looked at me and said in Dari, "This is Captain Edmanton." The woman heard this, shook her head, and spoke again. The translator continued. "She says her name is Mindy. I am Shiaraqa. We are very happy to meet you. You do not need to be afraid. Nobody will hurt you." Every time the woman spoke, Shiaraqa listened and then translated. "Captain Mindy wants to be your friend and help you. She is a medical officer and would like to see your mouth."

What? My mouth? Had these people traveled

all this way to look at my mouth? Was I so ugly that they had heard about me even in America? But I relaxed a tiny bit. At least they weren't here with the Citadel police.

Baba looked at me, raised his eyebrows, and circled his hands in a "hurry and show them your mouth" gesture. I looked over to Anwar and his friends to see if they were ready to scream out donkey sounds, but they were shaking hands with one of the soldiers on the other side of the trucks.

"It's okay," said Captain Mindy through her interpreter.

I lowered my chador. There, in front of the whole crowd and these soldiers, was my ugly split lip and my twisted teeth. My face felt hot with embarrassment.

The woman looked closely and said something that the interpreter did not translate. Then she turned and shouted to the nearest American. The soldier replied quickly and ran to one of the gun trucks. In a moment he returned and handed her a camera.

Instinctively, I brought my hand up to cover my face.

"Zulaikha, she needs to see your mouth," said Baba. He sounded very serious.

I willed my hands down to my sides and clenched the front of my dress. The camera flashed. Then again. After it had flashed several times, Captain Mindy smiled. "*Tashakor*." She moved beside me and put her arm around me, handing her camera to the soldier she had yelled at earlier.

The soldier slung his rifle around to his back as he took the camera, then nodded and said, "*One, two, three*," in a rough imitation of Dari before he pushed the button to take another picture.

Captain Mindy took the camera back, turned it around, and showed me the screen on the back. There was the picture with her arm around me. I had to let her squeeze me as she laughed, her pistol pressed against me. Then, after she said something in her language, Shiaraqa said, "Thank you for coming out here to meet us."

The woman spoke to the male soldier, and again he answered quickly and ran to the gun truck. She turned back to me, smiled, and spoke. Shiaraqa said, "We have some toys we would like you to have. If you are too big for them, maybe you know someone who could use them. Do you have any younger brothers or sisters?"

Did she really want me to talk to her? My hand

slipped up to cover my mouth. I looked up from the ground to the handgun at the woman's side.

"Zulaikha." Baba's voice was firm. "She asked you a question. Answer her."

"I have two little brothers," I said quietly.

Her translator told her what I'd said. She smiled again and took a box from the man whom she'd sent to the truck. I stared at him. Why was he doing everything Captain Mindy told him to do? Wasn't he angry with her for ordering him around? I certainly didn't like the way he kept smiling and looking at me.

The box was pretty big, and it was completely filled with brightly colored plastic toys, shiny metal toy cars, and candy in sparkly wrappers.

"Go ahead. Take some toys for you and your brothers. Have some candy too," said the interpreter.

I looked at Baba, whose mouth barely turned up toward something like a smile. He nodded at me, and so I reached into the box, shuffling the toys around, hardly aware of what I was choosing. I pulled out what looked like a toy soldier, but one that would make Khalid forget about his entire army of little tan army men. The one in my hand was about eight centimeters tall with movable arms and legs.

I shuffled back through the box, searching for another army man for Habib. I moved slowly and carefully, though. I didn't want the Americans to think I was greedy, and I didn't want Baba to have to spend very much money.

Shiaraqa looked at the two plastic soldiers in my hand. "Are you sure that is all you want? She says you should take some more." He nodded toward the captain.

But I already had so much. I shrugged my shoulders and looked down, forcing myself to remember patience. Maybe if I just waited long enough, everyone would let me go home.

"*Baksheesh*." Captain Mindy was telling me the toys were a gift. At least Baba wouldn't have to pay for them. She placed in my hands five different-colored sparkly hair clips. Then she dug down into the box again and produced a purple hairbrush. I could hardly hold it all. She spoke, but this time Shiaraqa translated very quietly and did not look at me. "She says it is a gift for your beautiful hair." He handed me a plastic sack for carrying the presents.

Captain Mindy reached up toward my hair and I flinched back. She smiled. Did she think it was funny to force a girl like me out of my house so that she could put me on display and dress me up like her doll?

She said something to the soldier who was with her. He pulled a small radio from his pocket and spoke into it. At once the other soldiers began checking over their weapons and equipment, moving closer to their trucks. The way the woman talked to the soldiers sounded just like Malehkah when she was ordering me about. No. She sounded like Baba. Her voice rang with authority. And when she spoke, the other Americans obeyed.

"*Khuda hafiz.*" She smiled at me and nodded to my father.

Then Captain Mindy and the soldier she'd been ordering around shook hands with all the Afghan men in the crowd. I watched in amazement as this woman reached out and shook Baba's hand. She must have thought it was perfectly okay to touch men who were not her husband or family. A few people in the crowd whispered to one another as they watched.

Waving with big, dumb smiles, the Americans all kept saying something that sounded like "*khuda hafiz*" as they climbed into their trucks. Then, with the soldiers behind the top guns still calling out goodbye, and a dozen kids chasing after them, the Americans drove away.

As we watched them go, Baba put his hand on my shoulder. I'd never seen this look on his face before, his mouth turned up in a sort of strange smile, but the expression in his eyes shifting. First happiness, then… What? Not fear, but not joy either. I looked at Najib, who shrugged and stepped up to put his hand on Baba's arm.

"Baba-jan, what did they want? What is all this about?" Najib moved his head from one side to the other as though trying to get Baba to see him. "Baba, what do they want with Zulaikha?"

Baba jerked and turned to Najib as though Najib had just woken him from a deep sleep. "Can you believe that? A woman. A woman officer." He ran his hand back, smoothing his hair. "They're supposed to be the most powerful army in the world, and they have women in command of men." He wiped the sweat from his brow. Then he smiled and slapped Najib on the back. "She says they want to fix Zulaikha's mouth. Make her teeth and lip right."

I must not have heard Baba correctly. He must have misunderstood them. I touched my teeth. Could they possibly put my teeth in a straight line like everyone else's? Could they give me a real lip?

How would they do that? There wasn't even really a lip there to fix. More important, if they were here to fight the Taliban and get revenge for the terrorist attacks on their own country, why would they fix my lip? How could it possibly help them?

"Baba, is this true?" I asked. Now I didn't know if I was dizzy from the heat, the excitement of rushing out to see the soldiers, or this impossible news.

Baba smiled with a slow nod. "She says it would cost us nothing. If their doctor in Kandahar believes he can fix your mouth, the Americans will provide the operation for free."

The American soldiers had doctors? Well, of course they did. How else would they fix up their men if one of them was hurt? But why would they use one of their busy doctors to help me? Surely, there were others who needed help more. Did it matter? If what Baba said was true, I might finally look normal. Najib patted me on the back and smiled at me.

Baba had a far-off look in his eyes again. As the crowd dispersed, he looked at the school construction project. "What did I tell you?" he said. "It's all working out for the best."

When Baba had talked about good times ahead, I had never even imagined that my greatest wish might come true. I put my hand to my mangled mouth. Maybe I could look nice in time for Najib's wedding. I squeezed the plastic sack in the tight grip of my sweaty hand.

"This is good news," said Najib.

"HA! It's great news! Nothing can go wrong for us!" Baba put his hand on my shoulder. "Don't worry." He squeezed me close to him. "You run along home, Zulaikha. I will make all the arrangements. Your baba will take care of everything."

8

"Oh, Zulaikha, that's wonderful! It's beyond wonderful. It's a miracle!" Zeynab threw her arms around me and kissed my cheek.

Back at home, my sister and I were talking on the roof of our house while Khalid and Habib played with their new toy soldiers. I had told Zeynab everything that had happened at the construction site.

"I never even knew something like this was possible." I sat down, resting my back against the wall at the edge of the roof. "I almost can't believe that such a miracle could happen. Is that a sin, Zeynab? To doubt so much when I should be dancing with happiness?"

Zeynab took a seat beside me and draped an arm over my shoulder. "Of course it's a sin." I looked at her and she laughed. "But Allah the most merciful will forgive you. I will even say extra prayers so that the surgery happens soon." She rocked us from side to side. "You're finally getting what you've always deserved. After this surgery, you'll be even prettier. One day, you'll be a wonderful wife for your husband."

I wished I could be fixed right now. Then I took a deep breath and reminded myself once again to be patient. To have faith. And I said a silent prayer, thanking Allah for this wonderful chance at this surgery, not to make me pretty like Zeynab, but to ease Baba and Malehkah's worries about finding me a husband. To finally end my days as Donkeyface.

We heard the heavy breathing that could only be Malehkah working her way up the stairs. Zeynab and I stood up. When Malehkah reached the roof, she leaned back against the door to the steps.

"Madar, you didn't have to come all the way up here. We would have come down if you'd called," said Zeynab.

Malehkah nodded and wiped her brow. "Are you okay?" she asked me.

My mouth fell open. "I'm sorry. What did you say, Madar?"

"Are you okay? The soldiers and everything."

"Bale, Madar." I really could not remember the last time Malehkah had asked about my well-being.

She looked down at her fingers, interlaced over

her belly. Then she nodded. "Good, because we have a lot of work to do before the guests arrive. You can start with the sitting room."

Zeynab shrugged and took my hand. Together we followed Malehkah downstairs.

I swept the floor of the sitting room as slowly and with as much control as I could, trying to push the dust out of the room without stirring up a sandstorm. The sitting room was a small chamber set apart from the house, next to the front compound wall. It had its own entrance, so that guests would not intrude in our private space. The room was meant to impress, but no matter how we tried to keep it sealed, the dust always found a way in. When I turned around to examine my work after more than an hour, the dust swirled in a column of light, settling back down to make all my efforts pointless.

"Why bother trying?" I slapped at the dirt with the broom.

The broom had brushed a swoop in the dust that reminded me of the letter *alif*. I peeked out the sitting room door to be sure I was alone. Then I sat down and used my finger to trace out letters in the dust.

I loved the way the lines, swoops, hooks, and dots of the letters took shape. The sounds they could make.

The feeling of making something all my own. I didn't know many words yet, but I smiled when I thought of all Meena could teach me and of the way she had recited the beautiful poetry. The ancient wonder that I had felt in the back of the sewing shop, that magic that floated in on the wind across the years. A connection to Madar-jan, maybe? I looked at my letters. They were getting better, but they were still clumsy. I needed to get back to Meena soon.

"What are you doing?"

I swept my hand over the floor, wiping out my writing, and spun around. Zeynab stood at the door, holding two rolled toshaks under each arm.

"I was just finishing."

She looked at me the same strange way she had that night after I'd met Meena. "Malehkah will want help inside." She came in and placed the toshaks around the room for the men to lean against. Then we went back across the courtyard and into the house.

"Sort rice." Malehkah pointed to a large tub. "And hurry. There's more to do after that's done." Zeynab and I went to the large rice bowl. "Not you," she shouted at Zeynab. "You go wash yourself. You're filthy after dusting the cushions."

Zeynab looked at me and shrugged, then went

to wash. I was filthy too. Grit clung to me, mixed with little runs of sweat. Why was Malehkah acting so crazy? We had prepared for Baba's business dinners with Hajji Abdullah in the past. They meant a little more work, mostly extra cleaning and more food to prepare, but they had never made Malehkah act like she was in such a hurry. She certainly never bothered with making sure any of us were clean before guests arrived. After all, the visitors would be in the sitting room. We would never even see them.

I glared at Malehkah, watching her frying the chicken and seasoning the mutton and beans. Then I wiped the sweat from my forehead and went back to work.

★ ★ ★

Hours later, while Zeynab put on her good dress, Malehkah called Khalid and me to the kitchen. She pointed out the order in which the various dishes should be served. "Leave the food in here, and covered, to keep the flies off. I will send Khalid out to get whatever we need."

"But Madar," I said. "Baba isn't even home yet."

"Zulaikha, just do as you're told!" She dipped

a rag in a basin of water and then wiped her brow. She walked past me and headed out to the front porch. "Come with me," she said. "We have to get your sister's hair fixed up."

"Bale, Madar," I said. What was happening? Something was very wrong.

When Zeynab joined us on the porch, Malehkah motioned her closer and then handed me two smooth green ribbons. I ran them through my fingers. Were they new? Malehkah dragged a brush through my sister's hair.

"Tie them," said Malehkah when she was finished brushing. While I tied the ribbons into bows in Zeynab's hair, Malehkah went to the kitchen and returned with a small sweet cake in hand. "Here," she said to Zeynab. "There was enough batter for me to make an extra cake. You should eat something."

A cake? Just for Zeynab? My sister looked at me and I shook my head. I didn't know what it meant either.

"Can Zulaikha have some?" Zeynab asked.

Malehkah shrugged and dropped her eyes. She rubbed her belly.

"Madar, are you okay?" Zeynab handed the cake to me and then reached out to take Malehkah's hand.

Malehkah pulled her hand away, but when she finally answered, her voice sounded changed. Smaller. Her usual abruptness and anger were gone. "When you are asked questions tonight, do not answer. Do not even look up. I will answer all the questions for you."

"I don't understand." Zeynab frowned. "Why would—"

"Come." Malehkah motioned toward the sitting room. She spotted Khalid in the doorway to the house. "Come along, both of you. The guests will arrive soon."

Zeynab looked at Malehkah, her eyes wide. Malehkah's eyes were shiny. She wiped them and nodded.

My sister hesitated. Then she took Khalid by the hand and both of them went with Malehkah across the front courtyard to the sitting room, leaving me to wait by myself. On my way back into the house, I ground the back of my hand against my teeth. What was happening?

Finally, after a long wait in the hot kitchen, Khalid returned with the cloth, pitcher, and water basin. Everyone in the sitting room had washed their hands and prayed. It was time for the meal.

"Madar wants me to bring the food," Khalid said. "I hope there's some left over for us. There are two women in there with Madar and Zeynab. One of them is really fat!"

I knew I should have scolded my brother for speaking badly about a guest, but I felt such a strange mix of relief and surprise that I had to steady myself against the shelves. Baba and Najib still hadn't come home, and I had been worried that Malehkah and my sister were alone in the sitting room with Hajji Abdullah. Instead they were talking with two women. Why?

I handed my brother a tray with the large bowl of rice, the plate of chicken, the mutton and beans, and lots of naan. "What are they talking about in there?"

Khalid shrugged. "The fat woman is asking a lot of questions."

"Questions about what?"

"I don't know. Things about cleaning and cooking." Khalid turned for the door. "Madar said I should hurry with the food."

I blew out a frustrated breath that whistled through my teeth.

"If there's food left, I'll bring some out so we can eat," Khalid shouted as he rushed out of the house.

But with Zeynab in the sitting room and no answers out here, food didn't sound as good as it usually did. It was one of the longest evenings of my life. I watched to make sure Habib stayed out of trouble. I waited. I washed a few of the pots in the kitchen. I waited. Out in the front courtyard, I paced back and forth in the dust as the evening light began to fade.

Finally, the sitting room door opened. Zeynab came out and closed the door behind her. Her hands shook, and though she smiled, a tear ran down her smooth cheek.

"Zeynab!" I whispered. "What happened? What did they want?" I reached my arm around her back and pulled her toward the house.

When we reached the middle of the courtyard, she finally spoke. "Zulaikha," she said. "I think… I'm… I think I'm going… going to be married."

A shudder went through me. My legs shook so much that I thought I would fall down. Zeynab was unsteady too. She turned toward me and we leaned our foreheads together as we held each other.

"Are you sure?" I asked.

"Yes."

My sweet sister would soon be married. Soon

she'd wear the dress that she and I had spent so long sewing. She'd have a great husband in a beautiful house where she could start a wonderful family.

"That's…" I wiped a tear from my eye and pushed away any bad thoughts about how lonely I'd be once she left. She was my sister and I had a duty to be happy for her. I was happy for her. "Oh, Zeynab!" I hugged her. "Aren't you excited?"

"Of course I am," said Zeynab. "I'm just… shocked, I guess. I didn't expect this so soon. When I overheard Baba talking about a bride-price, I just assumed he was talking about Najib's wedding. I never dreamed he was talking about me."

I couldn't wait. "Who is he? Baba-jan must have found you the perfect husband."

"He's a very good man. Wealthy. Respected." Zeynab fanned her face and blew out an exhausted breath. I guided her to the porch where we sat down together, my arm around her, holding her close. Finally, Zeynab went on. "He's Hajji Abdullah's brother. His name is Tahir."

My eyes went wide. Hajji Abdullah was old. Baba said he had a long white beard.

Zeynab must have seen my shocked expression. "Relax. Tahir is the hajji's youngest brother. He is only maybe forty-five or so."

"Only forty-five?"

I felt Zeynab shrug. "So he is not a young boy. That only means he knows what he wants and that he will be better able to take care of me. He's wise and strong and kind, and I will be the youngest and prettiest of his wives."

"He has—"

"Two other wives." Zeynab stood up. She spun around so that the skirt of her pretty pink and purple flowered dress fanned out. "But my new husband will love me. His other wives and I will be the best of friends. We'll all help one another. Anyway, Baba knows what's best."

"He loves you," I said. "He wouldn't let you get married to anyone who wasn't the perfect match."

"Exactly!" she said.

I did not know how I felt. This news was so unexpected. Strange and yet wonderful. "I'm so happy for you, Zeynab."

"He lives in Farah."

I looked at my sister. The city of Farah was over an hour away. How could I live so far apart from my sister?

"I know." Zeynab must have sensed my worry.

"But Baba has the car now and he and Tahir and Hajji Abdullah are doing so much work together here and in Farah. We'll be able to arrange lots of visits."

Maybe she was right. "I hope so," I said.

"Three weeks and I'll be married. The shirnee-khoree is next week!"

Such fast progress. It was unheard of to agree to the marriage and the date of the engagement party after only one meeting. "What? Why so soon?"

Zeynab circled her hand in the air. "Something about the arrangement of American construction contracts. All that bride-price stuff." She shrugged. "It's... not what I expected. Baba and Tahir had basically already agreed to everything. The meeting tonight was kind of a formality." Zeynab pushed a strand of hair back behind her ear. "But Hajji Abdullah is such a great man that he has offered to help his brother and me have the best wedding celebration." She smiled.

I stood up and rushed to my sister, throwing my arms around her. "I love you."

"Bale, sister. I love you more."

"Zeynab, go inside now and change your clothes. Zulaikha, help me wash the dishes." Malehkah had come out of the sitting room. The guests must have gone home. It was getting so dark I could hardly see her standing there in the shadows.

My sister turned away from me and looked at our father's wife. She rubbed her eyes. "Bale, Madar."

9

"Maybe getting married is a bad idea," Zeynab said. "It takes too much work."

It was a week later. We were sitting on the front porch, taking a moment to relax after working all day to get ready for the shirnee-khoree. In addition to our usual chores, we had to cook more than ever before. It was like making three or four regular meals, but beyond buying naan and cooking rice, chicken, and lamb, we also had to prepare sweets. All day the kitchen blazed hot as we baked cakes, roasted almonds for sugaring, and even made candy brittle. After that, we had to wash and get dressed. Tahir Abdullah had sent Zeynab a pretty lavender dress to wear for the night, and I tied purple ribbons in her hair.

Malehkah's sister Tayereh had arrived late in the afternoon with her husband, Uncle Ghobad, and Malehkah's mother Farida – too late to help prepare for the party. Now that Baba, Uncle Ghobad, and Najib had taken the boys to Hajji Abdullah's to celebrate with the men, and everything and everyone was ready for the shirnee-khoree, it felt good to enjoy some simple quiet time with my sister.

"Tonight will be great." I patted her back. "Just like we always dreamed about."

Zeynab stared straight ahead and nodded, her hands folded tightly in her lap. She looked beautiful with her makeup and the ribbons, but I could tell she felt nervous. "Anyway, at least we don't have to cook for the men tonight," I said.

"Or watch the boys. There's enough to worry about without having to look after them all night."

I shook my head. "There's nothing to worry about."

"What if the party doesn't go well? I mean, the Abdullahs are a big, rich family and we're just... Well, our family isn't as large. They won't even all be here tonight."

"That's fine for me," I said. Given the short notice, Baba's brother's family couldn't travel from Kabul in time for the shirnee-khoree. Uncle Ramin had stayed in the capital when Baba fled the fighting there just before I was born. He and his wife Halima and their daughter Khatira had visited only twice that I remembered, once shortly after Khalid was born and then again for Habib's birth. Each time Baba and Uncle Ramin had ended up shouting at each other over old arguments and new disagreements. Uncle had sent word through Hajji Abdullah's satellite phone that they would arrive in An Daral the night before the wedding. "I hate the way they always talk about how much better their precious, modern city life is in Kabul. Then Khatira always stares at my mouth and talks to me like I have some sort of deadly disease."

Zeynab laughed briefly. "What if the Abdullah family doesn't like me?"

I ran my hand down her arm, smoothing her beautiful dress. "How could anyone not like you?"

"Farida and Tayereh—"

"Malehkah's family doesn't like anyone. How do you think she became so mean?"

Zeynab laughed again. It was wonderful to see her smile.

Malehkah came out of the sitting room where she had been talking with her mother and sister. "It's time to go inside now."

Zeynab and I stood up and started for the sitting room, but Malehkah reached out her hand to stop us. "You both know that tonight's shirnee-khoree is a celebration of Zeynab's engagement to Tahir. More importantly, this is our chance to show her future family that she comes from the right background. Whatever you do tonight will say something about your father, so be sure that what you do says something good. Zulaikha, you will help me serve the food. You will speak only when spoken to, and then you will say as little as possible."

She turned to Zeynab. "You must not appear too sad, or else they will think you do not wish to join their family. Also, you must not seem too happy or you'll look like you are ungrateful and hate us. There will be singing and dancing later, but neither of you will join in." As usual, Zeynab and I just nodded and agreed with our father's wife. "Finally... " But then we heard giggling happy voices outside and a heavy knock on the compound door. Malehkah sighed, straightened her dress, and said, "Let's get this thing over with."

My sister nodded and started to lick her lips before she remembered the heavy red lipstick. She breathed deep and let it out before nodding again to Malehkah, who led us across the courtyard to the sitting room. While Zeynab settled onto the special couch Hajji

Abdullah had lent us for the occasion, I went through the room and into the small walled-in hallway that shielded the rest of our compound from the eyes of guests who visited by this door.

Someone rapped on the door again and a woman's voice called, "Salaaaaaaaaam."

I took a moment to smooth down my hair and dress before unlocking the door and swinging it open. In rushed about a dozen chadri-covered women, all giggling and chatting at once. None of them even seemed to notice me. They went directly into the sitting room where there were more bursts of high-pitched enthusiastic greetings. I closed and bolted the street door.

"Zulaikha!" Malehkah's voice sounded pleasant and cheerful for a change. But the familiar impatience was still there behind her words.

Inside, the women had already removed their chadris and taken their seats. Zeynab sat on her couch at one end of the narrow sitting room. Malehkah perched near the door to the front of the compound. Women of all ages sat on the floor and leaned on the cushions against the wall, forming a large circle. I sat down in the space reserved for me, near Malehkah and her mother and sister.

"So, *this* is the little angel. The one the Americans took such an interest in." A very large woman sat at the end of the oval of women, directly across from my sister. She leaned forward and peered at my mouth, then ran her hand back to smooth down her long gray hair. She had to be almost as old as Meena. "There certainly is some work to do. You poor thing. Do you really think the Americans can fix it?"

I didn't know how to respond, but remembering Malehkah's instructions, I simply nodded and then looked at the floor. Another woman, not much younger, but quite a bit smaller, reached over to touch the big one. "My dear, I think you're frightening the little one, examining her mouth the way you are."

"Of course." The woman smiled. "I'm Gulzoma, first wife to Hajji Abdullah. This is my husband's older sister Jamila."

"Salaam," I said quietly.

"This is my mother Farida," said Malehkah.

"Salaam alaikum," Gulzoma bowed in greeting.

"Walaikum salaam," Farida replied.

"And my sister Tayereh," Malehkah continued the introductions.

Jamila nodded toward a woman who was clearly missing a leg and who must have walked with the crutch that she propped against the wall next to her. "This is my daughter Isma."

Then Gulzoma shifted the mountain of her body back and pointed at all the other women, naming off Hajji Abdullah's second and third wives as well as several daughters and nieces. She had forgotten some of the names, bringing scowls from the faces of their mothers, who then had to help her. Malehkah greeted each woman in turn. Zeynab looked like she was trying to follow everything Gulzoma said. When I caught Zeynab's attention, I raised my eyebrows. She turned her eyes toward one woman after another and then shrugged with the smallest hint of a smile on her lips. I covered my mouth and tried to look serious. Zeynab must have been thinking what I was thinking. There were many names to remember!

Gulzoma leaned forward. "Tahir's wives, Leena and Belquis, send their apologies. They simply cannot make it tonight. The trip from Farah is over an hour. I'm afraid they don't travel well, the poor things." She shook her head.

This was unexpected. The shirnee-khoree was important enough for Malehkah's family to travel here from Shindand, so surely the rest of Tahir's household could have made the shorter trip to

An Daral. But Gulzoma laughed. "They're busy preparing for Zeynab's arrival. I've hired servants to get my house ready for the wedding, but *everyone* is needed to get my brother-in-law's house ready for the wedding night!"

Malehkah's breath was warm at the back of my neck. "Come with me. We need to start bringing out the meal," she growled quietly.

Gulzoma clapped her hands. "Yes, let's eat. I'm hungry and I'm sure Zeynab has prepared a wonderful meal."

"Of course," Malehkah's nod seemed to pump freshness back into her smile as she gently pushed me out of the sitting room.

We went across the courtyard and inside the house to get the food from where it stayed warm on the cook stove. Malehkah said nothing, but quickly handed me a large platter on which she placed bowls and plates of food. Under my arm she crammed the dastarkhan before she nodded toward the sitting room. I hurried back, set down the platter, and unrolled the long dastarkhan in the middle of the circle of women. It was good that we had moved quickly because the conversation was slow. They seemed to be waiting for us. Malehkah brought a pitcher of water, a metal basin, and a towel that I carried around so that everyone could wash their hands. After that, we laid all the food out on the cloth – all our hard work through the long day. First the naan, then four big bowls of rice. Two roast chickens for everyone to pick pieces off. Bowls of spiced mutton in heavy red gravy, along with two large platters of roasted potatoes. I even put out a few plates of pickled cucumbers.

Finally, I could sit down. The women all ate, talked, laughed, and ate some more. Even Malehkah seemed a bit less grumpy. I was quiet, and I didn't eat much. Gulzoma and the others were already staring at my mouth enough. I didn't want to make it worse by letting them see the strange way that I had to eat, tilting my head back and using my fingers to help hold the food in while I chewed. Instead I took food to Zeynab, who wasn't supposed to move around.

"How are you doing?" I whispered when I brought her some chicken and naan. Gulzoma was holding everyone's attention with a story about one of her nieces.

Zeynab accepted the food. "I think everything is going well. The food is delicious and—"

"Zulaikha!" Malehkah called me back to her side with a little jerk of her head.

"You look wonderful," I whispered to Zeynab. "And the party is great." Then I went back to sit next to my father's wife.

Gulzoma and Jamila dominated the conversation. They talked about their relatives and laughed about stories from weddings they'd been to in the past. They even had a few stories about Hajji Abdullah's second and third wives. Several of these stories made some of the women blush and keep their eyes focused on their food.

During a rare quiet moment while Gulzoma helped herself to a choice piece of chicken, Isma spoke in a high soft voice. "Zulaikha, I hope the Americans are able to help you."

Everyone in the room turned their attention on me. My face felt hot. I had been about to sneak a little bite of a piece of naan, but I put the food back down. "Tashakor," I said.

"Yes," Gulzoma pointed with a chicken leg at the woman. "Isma here no doubt wishes they could give her a new leg the way they said they could give Zulaikha a new mouth." She chuckled. "Too bad for her!"

Everyone else sat in silence at her rudeness. It was Malehkah who finally spoke. "Not a new mouth.

They simply wanted to fix the one she already has."
She smiled, but there was an unmistakable firmness
behind her words to Gulzoma.

Gulzoma looked at Malehkah and picked her
teeth with her fingernail. Then she went on as though
Malehkah hadn't said anything at all. "Well, let's
hope it works." She turned to a woman sitting at the
other end of the room near Zeynab. "What was it
that your spirited son used to call Zulaikha, Mariam?
Donkeymouth? No. Ah! Yes, of course. Donkeyface!"
She clapped her hands, as if she was pleased that
she'd remembered. Then she frowned and put a
finger to her lips. "What a mean little boy. You should
try harder to keep him in line."

My cheeks burned hot at the mention of that hated
name. I pressed my chador tightly over my mouth.
How could any guest be so cruel to her host?

Anwar's mother, Mariam, the young third wife
of Hajji Abdullah, looked down, picking at her food.
Gulzoma smiled and took more chicken. "Mmm,
Malehkah, this is wonderful." She noticed me staring
at her. "Zulaikha, you haven't got a new mouth yet,
dear. Now close it."

But my mouth was closed. As much closed
as it could be with my cleft lip. I wanted to throw

my water in that fat old lady's face.

"Zulaikha. Zeynab." Malehkah leaned back and held her hands over her belly. "Will you please go inside and get the tray of sweets?"

Gulzoma sat up straight. "Does Zeynab need to go? Surely Zulaikha can—"

"I think Zeynab needs some air. The heat and all," Malehkah said, locking eyes with Gulzoma, a cheerful smile pasted on her face.

"Oooh, this is my favorite part," Isma said in her tiny voice. "I love the sweets. What better way to begin an engagement?" Other women quickly voiced their nervous agreement.

"Bale, Madar," I said. I took Zeynab's hand in mine and went to the house.

"That was terrible!" Zeynab said as soon as we were inside. I quickly put my finger to her lips and checked to make sure nobody had followed us. "Zulaikha, she's a monster. How can I become a part of that family?"

I wished that she didn't have to. I wished that life could stay the same as it had always been. I reached toward Zeynab and wiped the tears from her cheek. "'Every triumph from patience springs, the happy herald of better things,'" I said.

Zeynab managed a small smile. "Madar-jan used to say that."

"I know. And she was right. Maybe we need to get the cake, candies, and fruit and then go back in there and be like Malehkah."

Zeynab laughed softly. "You mean, really angry all the time?"

I hugged my sister. "No. Just all smiley and nice to all of them. Maybe if we can trick them into thinking we like them, then they'll be more kind."

"I'll try." Zeynab took a deep breath.

Taking the sweet things from the kitchen, we went back to the stifling hot sitting room and our rude guests.

Zeynab took her seat on the couch, and I placed the platter of sweet treats before the others, careful to set it within reach of Gulzoma. All the women looked at the assortment and smiled or made longing noises when they recognized something they liked.

The conversation went on and on. Gulzoma, Jamila, Mariam, or one of the others would ask Farida or Tayereh questions. Answers would follow. Farida would ask something else. Someone would answer. Mixed into this would be the occasional family story, usually told by Gulzoma or Jamila. Several times

I saw some of the Abdullahs staring at my mouth. Some of them even looked and then whispered to each other, looks of pity or disgust on their faces. I found myself wishing these people would leave.

Finally, a long car horn sounded outside the compound. Gulzoma put her hands on her hips and frowned. "Ah, that must be the men come to take us home."

"Leave it to them to put a stop to all the fun," said Jamila.

Gulzoma stood up. It was a signal to everyone else to do the same. She beamed at Malehkah. "Tashakor. Such a wonderful night!" Other women agreed and offered compliments, but Gulzoma didn't seem to notice them. "Zulaikha, you poor little thing." She took my face in her hands and peered at my mouth. I did my best to look as though it didn't bother me. "Maybe the Americans *can* fix this. Maybe even in time for the wedding? Ooh." She let go of me, shook her head, and wiped her hands on her dress. "I certainly hope so." Chadris were passed around from where they were piled in the corner. "Zeynab, you are absolutely beautiful. Tahir is such a lucky man. Khuda hafiz!" Gulzoma led the party of chadri-covered women out of the compound, where cars waited to take them all home.

When Tahir's family had all gone, I pressed my chador over my mouth hard, staring at the door after them so that Malehkah's family wouldn't see the tears welling up in my eyes.

"Hey," Zeynab whispered. She stood behind me with her hand on my shoulder.

"Girls, make sure the dishes are done before you go to bed," said Malehkah. I heard her talking with her mother and sister as they headed back to the house.

"Are you okay?" Zeynab asked.

Her touch comforted me. It helped me remember what was really important tonight. I smiled the best I could and turned to face my sister. "I'm fine."

"But Gulzoma—"

"Is lucky she doesn't have to do all these dishes." I put my arm around Zeynab. "Come on." We started the long task of cleaning up after the shirnee-khoree.

10

Early the next morning, after Malehkah's family had driven back to Shindand, Zeynab and I went to work cleaning the sitting room before the day's terrible heat set in. I would never have imagined that women could be so messy. They'd spilled a surprising amount of the spiced mutton sauce. Worse, cake crumbs and a few orange peels were starting to draw ants.

Zeynab dipped her rag in the bucket of soapy water and slopped it on the floor. "You always hear women say that engagement and marriage are supposed to be so magical, but for a while last night, everything felt pretty tense."

"Well." I doused my rag in the now-dirty soapy water and scrubbed at a spot of dried red spice sauce. I wished there was a way I could just forget the stares and Gulzoma's thinly disguised cruelty. Even if I couldn't, it was my job to make Zeynab happy. "It all worked out for the best."

Zeynab wiped the sweat from her brow.

"At least I'm not being matched to that horrible Anwar." She laughed.

I frowned and shook my head. I could not join her in her little joke. Anwar was mean and scary, not funny.

Cold water splashed the back of my neck and I jumped up. "Zeynab!"

My sister giggled, shaking with laughter as she held the rag up to cover her big grin. "You deserve it, Little Miss Gloomy."

"How could I be gloomy?" I said, trying to shove aside any unpleasant thoughts. "You're getting married, and I may actually get my mouth fixed. What could be better?"

"I'll miss you so much, and…" Her eyes were wild and I knew she was dreaming up a thousand possibilities. "And I wish maybe my husband will have a handsome hardworking cousin or someone. Isma was nice. Maybe she has a son. Or Baba-jan could match you up with someone else in my husband's family." She wrung out her rag and wiped her brow. "Then maybe you and I could live together. Raise our kids together."

It was the old fantasy. I went and put my arm around my sister. Whenever Zeynab used to talk like this, I would always shake my head. After all, who would want to marry a girl with a mouth like mine? But now, I dared to dream along with my sister.

"It's all incredible," said Zeynab. "You'll have your surgery and then you'll be even more beautiful. You'll be worn out cleaning and cooking for all the people who want you to marry their sons." She took a deep breath, as if trying to calm herself. "Anyway," she said, "we must have faith that life will all work out. Inshallah, Zulaikha."

"Inshallah." I smiled back. God willing.

For a long moment, it was very quiet in the hot sitting room.

Finally, Zeynab looked into the bucket. "This water is no good. Whatever soap was in it is dead now. We're not doing anything but getting the dirt wet and stirring it around on the floor. I'll get fresh water."

"No," I said. "I'll get it." I was surprised that the water was so dirty already. I had put in all the soap we had left. It was part of my plan to see Meena again.

Malehkah glared at me suspiciously when I said we were out of soap, but she finally handed over the money and sent me to the bazaar. After she'd given me her usual warnings to behave and to hurry, I headed down the street with a smile that I hoped wouldn't be twisted for much longer.

✦ ✦ ✦

"Ah, child, I was wondering when I would see you again," Meena said in her worn leather voice as I entered her sewing shop. "I'm glad you've come. I was just about to take a break. Join me for a cup of tea?"

I helped her hang a bolt of fabric on a wooden rack before she led me back to her apartment. I felt as though I'd slipped back in time. Nothing had changed. The same small apartment. The same cup of tea. And Meena's same warm smile.

Letting go of my chador, I took a sip of my tea, using the cup to cover my mouth. Somehow she'd steeped the tea at just the right temperature, so I could throw back my head to keep the tea in my mouth without burning myself. It tasted wonderful, spicy and sweet. She didn't seem to even notice the strange way I had to drink.

"So your sister is engaged." The teacher sat on her bed again, one hand to her back and the other carefully steadying her cup. "And the Americans want to operate on your mouth."

I looked up from my tea. How could she have known all that? She shook with a soft laugh. "You don't need to look so mystified, child. Gossip travels fast, especially among the women for whom I sew. You must be excited."

I wasn't quite used to open talk with anyone but my sister. "I am excited. It's all so wonderful." I took another sip. "I never knew that anyone could do anything for my mouth. Now the Americans come and tell me they will fix it. It is... I..."

I didn't know what else to say. We both drank in silence.

Finally, Meena spoke. "Tell me, child, why do you want this surgery?"

"Why?" I nearly choked on my tea. I checked to make sure she wasn't teasing me. "I want to be normal. I don't want to look like a baby bird when I eat. I want—"

"To be like everyone else?"

"Yes! If I didn't have this..." I motioned to my mouth with my free hand "... then I wouldn't talk wrong like I do. Then maybe Malehkah wouldn't be so mean to me, and she and Baba wouldn't have as much trouble finding me a husband one day.

Maybe I wouldn't be so much of a burden." I thought of the way I'd felt last night when Gulzoma and everyone had paid so much attention to my split lip and crooked teeth. If I had looked normal, the party might have been more fun. I wiped my eyes with my chador, surprised that I'd said so much. Surprised that I was crying.

Meena stood up and crossed the room. She took a cloth bundle down from a shelf on the wall. When she returned, she held the bundle in her lap like a baby. "Your mother never thought you were a burden." Meena pulled back the old cloth. Inside was an ancient-looking book with a leather cover. She carefully opened the book, sliding her hands down the delicate pages. I watched the graceful swirls of letters between her fingers. "Your mother loved literature. But she loved you more. She wanted you to know both of her loves."

"I remember," I whispered.

She handed me a pencil and a small sheet of paper on a board. "Show me." She spoke gently.

"I only know a few words," I said. "But I've been practicing my letters."

"Good!" She smiled. "That's a start."

"Bale, Muallem-sahib." It felt right, somehow,

to call her my teacher. She closed her eyes with a contented look on her face, gently placing her hand on my arm to encourage me.

I wrote my letters and the few small words I could remember. *Cow. Wall. Moon. Love. Zulaikha.* I tried to think of more.

"Good," she said in a low, quiet voice. "That's very good after so long. Your memory is excellent." She showed me a page of the book. "Now, child, copy these words. Do not worry if you cannot understand it all. By copying the page again and again, you'll make the link between the sounds of the letters and the words they form. You'll understand in time."

She read the lines out loud, tracing her finger from right to left along the words as she read them, first slowly as I copied, then once more, faster, so that it all began to make sense. On her third reading, she asked me to say the words with her, keeping time with her finger. Then we read it together again, and I could tell we were both losing ourselves in the language:

All you who dwell in gardens of the young,
Don't waste your life in merriment and song.
Instead let sadness fill your tender soul
As you reflect on all you can't control:

How many joyous springs just come and go
And falling flower petals turn to snow,
And all humans understand they must
One day lie down forever in the dust.
Still people fight, and even clash with friends.
Fathers and sons both come to saddest ends,
And blood that family shares is too soon spilled.
Death brings no peace – just vengeance for the killed.
The gold in nature gets lost in the Fall;
The winter raids the fruit, devouring all.

"It's sad," I said, when we finished our last reading. "It's about sadness and sorrow."

Muallem nodded. "It is about endings and death. And yet, Firdawsi's epic *Shahnameh* has lived for over a thousand years."

I wanted to explain the way I felt when I heard her read the old poem, but I was not good with words the way Muallem was. "It's sad," I repeated. "But… the words have a pretty sadness."

"Indeed, they do, child."

"When I hear them… I feel an ache" – I put my hand over my heart – "right here. But at the same time, I want to hear more."

I looked down at the words I'd written on

the paper. Words that were at once a thousand years old and yet completely new. I held them to my chest, but did not feel foolish for doing so. Somehow I felt Muallem would understand. My mother could write and read this poem and more. I wanted to learn to do that too.

A car honked from a few streets away and I jumped. When I looked at my muallem, she looked startled as well. We both laughed.

"I need to go," I said.

"You'll be missed at home," said Meena. "Practice copying the words. Think of the sounds of the letters and the words as you copy. Start on the back of the paper, then find a way to practice over and over. Use a rock on cement. Trace the words in the dust."

I stuffed the paper and little pencil into the pocket of my dress. "Tashakor."

Meena smiled, clapping her hands together once. "You were born to be a great student. It is your destiny."

I rushed to buy the soap as quickly as I could, then I took the back roads home to avoid Anwar. When I scrambled, out of breath, into the central room of our house, my legs shook and my hands trembled. Malehkah was stroking Habib's hair, trying to get the little one to lie down for a nap.

She looked up at me and scowled. "That took you a long time. Go help your sister. She's out the back, beating the dust from the toshaks."

"Bale, Madar!" I hurried for the door.

In the back courtyard, Khalid was doing his best to help Zeynab in one of the only chores he would agree to do. She had hung the floppy red sitting-room cushions over the clothesline and was using the stick of our only broom to beat the dust out of them. Khalid made fighting noises as he tried to kick and punch the dirt from a toshak on the end.

"Let me help you," I greeted my sister.

She took a few steps toward me. "What took you so long? Where did you go?"

"I just… the crowd. There were a lot of people there. And the bargaining took forever." The words came out of my twisted mouth almost before I had decided to lie. It was the very first time I had ever truly lied to my sister.

I told myself that I couldn't let her know the truth. She thought it was a waste of time for girls to go to school. Of course she would disapprove. She probably wouldn't tell Baba. She certainly wouldn't involve Malehkah. But I still worried that if anyone else knew about my visits with Meena and about my lessons, I might lose my chance to learn. I didn't want all of that taken away from me before I'd even really explored it. Meena and her lessons and the poetry were all mine.

Zeynab narrowed her eyes and frowned, handing me the broom and pulling a toshak off the rope. She didn't say anything for a moment. She just looked at me. Then suddenly she laughed, whipped the toshak through the air, and beat me with it.

"Hey!" I waved the dust from my face. "You're dewana."

We worked the rest of the morning like nothing had changed for either of us, talking and laughing and doing our best to make our chores into games.

I was patching part of the front compound wall with Torran's dung when Baba and Najib came home later that afternoon. They looked sweaty and tired, with black smears and dirt on their clothes, but Baba had a sparkle of happiness in his eyes. He and Najib stopped near me.

"Zulaikha," said Baba. "I spoke with Hajji Abdullah this morning at the construction site. He says his brother Tahir talked to the Americans. They were so excited that they had Tahir call the hajji on

125

his satellite telephone with the news. The Americans have arranged for a helicopter to fly you to Kandahar for your surgery in one week."

Kandahar? In all this talk of my surgery, nobody had mentioned having to travel all the way to Kandahar. Certainly there had been no talk of flying there!

Baba must have seen the worry in my expression. He gently tilted my face up to look at him as he smiled big. "Hajji Abdullah himself has offered to oversee the job site here in An Daral while I am away. I will drive you to Farah and then go all the way to Kandahar with you! It will be a great adventure!"

"Bale, Baba." I put one hand over my mouth and the other over my pounding chest. Did I hear him correctly? Just one week? That would mean I could have a normal mouth in time for Zeynab's wedding. I could be done with my donkey face next week! Allahu Akbar! What could I say to my wonderful father for this miracle? I threw myself at him and wrapped my arms around him. "Tashakor."

My tired father put his arms around me. His head rolled back as he almost shouted with laughter. He laughed so hard, he had to dab at tears in the wrinkles at the corners of his eyes. "Wah wah, Zulaikha."

He patted my back. "Didn't I tell you your baba would take care of everything?" He tilted my chin up again and looked at me. Then he spoke to me very quietly, just to me. "You'll be so pretty."

I didn't want the moment to end.

11

Though of course she never showed it, Malehkah must have been happy with me through the whole next week. I rushed to milk Torran, to wash the clothes, to water the garden, to do any work that possibly needed doing. I had most of the chores completed before she even asked. I didn't want to upset anyone or do anything that might risk my chance at getting my mouth fixed.

Finally, the longest week of my life was over, and after a sleepless night, I was up first the next morning. After goodbyes and good wishes from everyone, even from Malehkah, Baba and I were on our way to Farah in the white Toyota.

This was my first trip out of An Daral, and my first ride in a car. I sat in a cushioned seat in what seemed like a little moving room and felt the vibrations from the motor shake through me. As we bounced down the road, I steadied in my lap the cloth-wrapped bundle of naan that Malehkah had given me before we left. I held on even tighter to the plastic handle in the door, trying to brace myself against every bump.

Baba saw me and smiled. "Don't worry. The road will smooth out when we get to the open desert. I'll show you how fast your father's Toyota can go!" He slapped a button in the middle of the steering wheel and the car beeped. "Now give your Baba a piece of naan. This adventure is making me hungry already."

I tore off a strip of bread and handed it to my father. He shook his head, leaned over, and growled playfully as he bit into the bigger piece of naan instead. I had to pull the loaf away to tear off the piece he had his mouth on. He laughed and then spoke while chewing. "Tashakor."

"You're welcome." I giggled.

Soon enough, we came to open land, and the road leveled out as promised. I'd never seen the world beyond the mountains that surrounded An Daral before. Barren grayness stretched out as far as I could see. Baba-jan sped up, humming an old tune. Once he looked at me quickly, then turned forward again. Then he looked back at me. He took a deep breath, but then pressed his lips together and breathed out through his nose. Finally, he spoke. "I'm glad you have the chance to have this operation, Zulaikha, even if we have to endure that American woman. You…" He trailed off and busied himself scraping a speck of dirt off the steering wheel. "You remind me very much of your mother. With your mouth all better, you'll look like her. More than Zeynab even. You're a good daughter. I'll always take care of you. So don't be frightened today."

All morning, I'd tried not to appear scared, but Baba-jan knew me too well. I hoped he also knew how happy his kind words made me feel.

I watched the rocky flats of the empty desert and wondered at the changing view of the mountains for a long time. After the car settled into a rhythm of rises and dips on the smooth ground, my eyelids felt droopy. The quiet rumbling of the car, the soft seat, and my father's reassuring presence made me feel safe. Safe and sleepy.

✦ ✦ ✦

Baba-jan woke me up as we pulled into Farah. I looked in amazement at an endless row of shops that lined both sides of a long, paved road and sold everything, including lots of items that were unavailable in An Daral. We even passed a bookstore! Meena would have loved that. Following Hajji Abdullah's directions, we went through a police checkpoint and turned down the dirt track that was supposed to lead to the American base.

"We're almost there, Zulaikha!" Baba slapped the steering wheel with a grin. "Ha! And as soon as I've finished my work on the school, I'll be coming this way all the time to work on the American base."

Baba's excitement mirrored my own. It wouldn't be long before my smile was just as good as anyone else's. He saw me grin, and laughed, giving my shoulder a squeeze.

But as he drove on for a while, he grew more and more tense. "Now where is that base?" he said, leaning down and looking intently out the windshield. "Hajji Abdullah said to turn left at the police checkpoint after the bazaar. He said it was impossible to miss."

We passed a cemetery, a rocky field with hundreds of stone mounds, each about the size of a person. There were many short mounds for children and babies. Then came a big field where the ground was slick with what must have been spilled gasoline or oil as men filled huge drums from trucks. Hundreds, maybe thousands of these fuel and oil drums were stacked up all over. One man puffed on a cigarette while he worked a hand crank to pump fuel from one big metal drum to another.

"Look at that ignorant slob." Baba shook his head. "Smoking away, and everywhere gas and oil. Some day he will blow up the whole place!"

I folded my hands tightly in my lap at the irritation in my father's voice. Baba was a wonderful man, but when he became upset, he could explode too. In my heart, I asked Allah to let the rest of our trip go smoothly and well, to let nothing go wrong on this day of my dreams. Baba gripped the steering wheel so tightly that his hands shook.

We followed the road out into the flats, where the people of Farah must have dumped everything they could not use or at least burn. Flies buzzed everywhere, and despite the heat, Baba closed the vents against the dusty rotting smell.

"If the base is out here, the Americans need to rethink where they build," said Baba.

We passed fields of brick fragments, piles of scrap metal, and bits of broken glass shining in the sun. I felt a twinge of unwanted, out-of-place sadness, being in this depressing, forgotten area on such a wonderful day.

The Toyota whined as it struggled up a hill.

And there it was. In the distance, rising up from the garbage, was an enormous compound.

"*Finally,*" said Baba.

The white, windowless walls of the American base rose into a square, standing just a little higher than our compound walls at home. A big red gate was in the middle of one of the walls. Four square white towers with windows formed each corner. As we approached, I could see a coiled wire fence looped around the entire fortress, set far away from its walls. Just inside the fence, the Americans had dug a deep ditch.

"Baba, look!" I pointed. "The Afghan and American flags together." The two flags flapping in the wind on tall poles above the middle of the base had to be a good sign. I felt my heart lift a bit.

"Quiet, Zulaikha! We have to be serious now." Baba squinted his eyes as he turned the car onto the track that led to the gate. "From now on, you will be quiet and do exactly as I say."

"Bale, Baba."

We drove alongside the razor-wire fence until we came to a gate, where Afghan police guards in gray uniforms stopped us. One of these men walked up to Baba's window with his gun slung easily at his side.

"Salaam. May I help you?" The guard spoke with a heavy Pashto accent. He couldn't have been much older than Najib.

"We…" Baba's voice almost squeaked. He licked his dry lips and started again. "We've come to see the female doctor. She came to An Daral and told us that the Americans could help my daughter." I turned away while the guard leaned in to look at me. "Tahir Abdullah spoke to the Americans about this last week," Baba added in a rush.

The guard smiled, nodded, and stood upright. He pulled a small radio from his pocket. "Interpreter, interpreter, this is front gate."

After a short burst of static a man answered, *"Go ahead."*

The guard told our story to the man on the radio.

"One minute. I'll ask the soldiers."

The guard with the radio beckoned for another soldier to join him. Then he bent down to speak to my father again. "They will probably let you in, but you'll have to leave your car out here."

Baba's eyes widened and he looked ahead at the base in the distance.

Radio Guard laughed. "I know it's a long walk. Sorry. I have my orders."

Baba parked the Toyota and we both climbed out. We waited in the hot sun for a few minutes. Baba looked at Radio Guard, who shrugged. Finally, his radio squawked.

"Let them come up. Tell them the captain is on her way out," said the man on the other end of the radio. *"Tell them the Americans are very happy they have come."*

"Bale," said Radio Guard.

"I heard him," said Baba.

Radio Guard chuckled and motioned for his comrade to pull the small coil of wire out of the way. He waved us through the gate. "Welcome to Farah Base."

To get to the base, we had to walk down a long, narrow lane between two coils of razor wire. The wind whipped up the dust, and I covered my face and closed my eyes against the grit. My father sighed and then licked his lips. "Stay close to me," he said quietly. "Stay close to me and do not speak unless I tell you to." I wanted to tell him that it was all right, that I didn't mind the walk. I would have walked all the way from An Daral for a chance to have a normal face.

Suddenly, my chador pulled back off of my head.

It had snagged in one of the sharp barbs on the coil of wire. Baba began to reach for it, but I quickly squeezed in between him and the wire. He'd pull too hard and rip my favorite chador. Besides my special white Eid chador, I only had two, and my other one was a drab dark blue. This pretty pink one was much better. The bright color drew people's attention away from my mouth.

"Hurry!" Baba growled. "I told you to stay right by me!"

Moving as gently as I could, I pulled my shawl off the wire and wrapped it around my body. I walked beside Baba as we made our way up the narrow path, careful not to get snagged again by the sharp steel teeth. As we neared the base, the walls seemed to loom even higher, another spring of sharp razor wire perched on top. The voice on the radio had said they were happy we'd come. If that was so, I'd hate to be here if they were angry.

The path widened to nearly three meters when we were about ten meters from the gate. Finally, two Americans stood up from a bench in the shade of the wall.

"*Salaam, rafiq!*" It was the African soldier I'd seen before. He had a big smile and warm eyes on a face as dark as my other shawl. I was surprised by how much smaller he looked without his body armor and helmet. He slung his rifle around his back and reached out to shake hands with Baba.

Shiaraqa, the interpreter, smiled next to him. "This is Corporal Andrews," he said. Then he translated for the corporal. "He welcomes you to Farah. He says the captain is very happy you're here."

Corporal Andrews crouched down and held out his hand to me. I remembered what my father had said and I pulled close to Baba's side. I felt him squeeze my shoulder and I looked up to see him nod in the direction of the corporal's outstretched hand. I hoped the soldier didn't notice me shaking as I reached out to him. He gently shook my hand and smiled again. It was the first time I had touched a man who was not a member of my family. I prayed I had understood Baba correctly and he wouldn't be angry with me for accepting the handshake.

Shiaraqa watched as though my touching a strange man was completely normal. He must have been accustomed to outrageous American behavior.

A second soldier approached, this one wearing armor on his chest and back but without a helmet. He shook my father's hand and then extended his hand to me. Again, I had to shake hands with a strange man. But this one was quiet, not like Corporal Andrews.

Shiaraqa translated for the corporal again. "Corporal Andrews says he is very sorry, but his friend must search people before they can enter the base. He says he does not like to do it, but his commanders force him to."

My father said nothing but nodded as the light-skinned soldier motioned to a little cement wall. There were three bags of sand on the ground, and Baba-jan was asked to place his hands against the wall while he spread his legs with his feet between the bags. I watched as the second soldier began to touch him all over. He patted his hands on each side of both of Baba's legs, up and up until his hands were too high. Why did they do this? Surely, no one would keep a weapon in that place. The soldier felt around Baba's waist. I looked away. My hands and feet sweated. The Americans seemed to have no idea how to treat people, especially how to treat girls. If they insisted on shaking my hand, would they also want to search me like they were searching my father?

So much wire everywhere. There was exactly one way out, back the way we had come in, but if I ran, the guards at the outer fence would catch me anyway.

Finally, they finished the search. Baba stepped close and put his arm around me. It was my turn, but I didn't care what was at stake. I absolutely would *not* allow this soldier to put his hands all over me.

"You can go in now," said Shiaraqa.

Did that mean I didn't have to be searched? Maybe I was too young. Maybe they'd forgotten. Maybe there was a shred of decency in them and they wouldn't touch a girl all over the way they'd felt my father.

"You do not need to search my daughter?" Baba said. I looked at him. Why did he have to ask that?

"What did he say?" Corporal Andrews asked in strange-sounding Dari.

The interpreter smiled and answered him in English. The American laughed and reached down to a pocket on the side of his pants. He pulled out two candies in shiny gold wrappers and held one out to my father and one to me, smiling as he said something. The Afghan translated Corporal's words. "We do not search angels at the Farah base."

I breathed with relief as we followed them. He should not call me an angel, but anything was better than letting him touch me like that. For people who called us *rafiqs*, they certainly didn't treat us like trusted friends.

We were led through the massive steel gate with its sharp metal spikes sticking straight up from the top. It clanged shut behind us. We were inside now. In the private world of the Americans. Somehow, the place looked even larger from within. To our right was a big metal tower with water tanks mounted on top. One soldier sprayed water from a hose while others used rags to wash their big truck. Outside another building, more men were busy changing the tire on a different vehicle. A few more soldiers ran next to the wall, wearing only black short pants and gray shirts. They were the only men on this busy base who had no guns.

There were at least five big buildings, with more under construction, all of them painted tan. They had built a whole village.

"Ah. Here she comes," said Shiaraqa.

A little red truck pulled up and out stepped Captain Mindy. Like Corporal Andrews, she looked much smaller without her armor and helmet, yet even inside the base, she still wore a pistol at her side.

"*Salaam!*" said the woman. I guess all American soldiers knew at least that one word. She held out her hand for me to shake and I looked up to my father. This was terrible. She must shake Baba's hand first, not mine. But she simply smiled and kept her hand extended. It was a great relief when my father nodded permission. Still, I felt like I was betraying Baba, insulting him by being greeted first.

Captain Mindy spoke and Shiaraqa translated. "She welcomes you. She says she is sorry that she did not learn your names the last time she saw you."

"Sadiq Frouton," my father said in a quiet voice. "This is my daughter Zulaikha."

"Zulaikha?" said Captain Mindy. She continued talking with a smile and her hand over her heart.

"She says Zulaikha is a lovely name," said Shiaraqa. He motioned toward the truck. "If you will climb in, she will take us to the medical room."

Baba and I crawled into the tiny back seats of the small vehicle, while Shiaraqa sat up front and Captain Mindy drove us across the base. We passed one of the construction sites, where dozens of Afghan men were hard at work on a new building. Nearby, two soldiers threw a big, brown, egg-shaped ball with pointed ends back and forth. Baba didn't seem to notice them. He stared straight ahead, his hands folded tightly in his lap and his eyes narrowed.

Finally, we stopped near the double doors of another tan building. Several meters away, seven Afghan men worked with pickaxes and shovels, carving a trench almost a half-meter deep. Near the trench, a soldier stood guard with his weapon hanging by its strap from his shoulder.

Baba leaned forward toward Shiaraqa and spoke quietly. "Why are the workers guarded?"

The interpreter shrugged. "They are digging to bury some electrical cables for the new barracks. The Americans are worried the workers will steal the tools."

Baba sat back in his seat and cracked his knuckles.

We climbed out of the truck and were led inside the building. It took a moment for my eyes to adjust to the dimness inside. We went a short way down the hall and then into what must have been their medical room. The floors, walls, and ceiling were white-painted cement. A large wooden desk occupied the corner. In the middle of the room were two wooden beds, and between those was a cart loaded with strange machines and equipment. Captain Mindy brought out two plastic chairs.

"She asks you to please sit down," said Shiaraqa.

I waited, watching over my chador to see what Baba would do. Without a word, he sat down in one of the plastic chairs and motioned for me to sit as well. I sat down, but first I pulled my chair a little closer to my father's. Captain Mindy took a seat on one of the wooden beds. Shiaraqa remained standing, but leaned against the wall.

Shiaraqa translated for Captain Mindy. "She has some bad news." I pressed my hand to my mouth. "The helicopter cannot make the flight from Kandahar. They say the weather is too bad."

As soon as the interpreter spoke, my shaking shoulders dropped. I slumped down in my chair and pulled my chador more tightly over my mouth. My father shifted position and cleared his throat. His words were short, clipped, and controlled, and the quiet in his voice frightened me like the stillness before a storm. "The weather is fine outside. It is hot, but not too windy. Why can't the helicopter make it?"

When Shiaraqa finished translating his words, Captain Mindy rolled her eyes and held up her hands, talking to Shiaraqa. He turned toward us. "She says she does not know why they have decided they cannot fly. Maybe it is the weather up in the mountains. She does not make this choice."

I watched my father clench his fists in his lap. The captain must have noticed his tension because her voice became louder and her words seemed to come more quickly. She shook her hands in front of her chest. Shiaraqa said to us, "No. You must not worry. There is another flight in one week."

Baba shook his head. "I have to work. I have asked engineer Hajji Abdullah to supervise my job site so that I could take this trip, and now it is for nothing. She said the helicopter would be here *today*!" He smacked his hand on the handle of his chair. Captain Mindy started talking to Shiaraqa, but Baba didn't give him the chance to translate. "The most powerful army in the world and they can't land a helicopter on a clear day? Or maybe this woman doesn't know when the helicopter is supposed to come."

"*What he say*?" Captain Mindy spoke urgently in bad Dari to Shiaraqa.

Shiaraqa started to translate, but Baba grabbed his arm and turned the interpreter back to face him. "Tell her, I have traveled a long way. She needs to do the surgery here herself. Today." He did not even look at the woman.

When Captain Mindy heard the translation, she

laughed and shook her head. My father quickly stood up. His plastic chair scraped back on the cement floor. A cold, dull emptiness dropped in my stomach. Shiaraqa looked at the floor, but translated the captain's words. "She does not have the training or the equipment to do the surgery here."

Captain Mindy started talking again with Shiaraqa translating, something about how this surgery was routine for the American doctor at Kandahar, but my father was already on his feet. Maybe the doctors would have no trouble with my mouth, but Captain Mindy didn't seem to understand that she had insulted my father. How dare she laugh at him and then go on with her plans like everything was fine? I looked at Shiaraqa, hoping he would explain this problem to the woman.

"She hopes you will return in one week so that—"

"I cannot come back in one week. The helicopter was supposed to come today! I do not get my money from my government like she does. I must work for it. I cannot afford to keep making these trips and missing work." He punched his fist into his palm. "She said that helicopter would be here today! These damned infidel Americans think we are all simple-minded." He tapped his finger to the side of his head. "Child minds, that we will just do whatever they say. They want us to pat them on the back for invading our homeland. They act like our friends, but I see the soldiers with their rifles guarding the workers outside. I felt their hands checking me for bombs. That's their friendship! Their trust! I know. Our family will be busy with wedding plans in a week. You tell her that we won't be back."

I felt an ache in the back of my throat and a stinging in my eyes.

Shiaraqa told Captain Mindy what my father had said, and her smile faded.

"She doesn't understand why you can't find someone to bring the girl next week so she can have the operation." Shiaraqa translated the captain's words, but he sounded like a puppet, not happy at all about what he had to say.

My father folded his arms over his chest and glared at Shiaraqa.

Captain Mindy repeated some of what she'd said earlier, but with greater emphasis. Shiaraqa shook his head and started to say something back to her. She snapped her fingers at him. I felt my father straighten up next to me. Finally, Shiaraqa sighed and spoke to me. "She says you are very beautiful and when we get this little problem taken care of, you will be a little princess."

My father breathed out a deep sigh that almost sounded like a growl.

I looked at my baba-jan, praying to Allah that he could fix this the way he could fix his car or a broken hinge on a door at home. Instead, he only silently stared at Shiaraqa. The surgery, my one hope in the world to be normal or even a little pretty, all the fantasies about a some-day happy marriage, none of it was going to happen. Those dreams belonged to my beautiful sister. I would be Donkeyface for ever. I'd always be stared at and pitied. I'd never be free of the cruel comments and humiliations from people like Gulzoma. When I saw her at the shahba-henna and the day after that at the wedding, she'd treat me like a monster on display for the guests.

Anwar had been right all those times he'd shouted at me. I was ugly. I would always be ugly. But now I knew he was right about something else too. I was ugly and stupid. Stupid to have ever believed that life could be any better. Stupid to trust the Americans.

Captain Mindy broke the long quiet. "Here." Shiaraqa put the American woman's eager words into our language. "You remember the corporal who was

147

at the gate today? He is the one who told us about you. He wanted you to have these little presents." From a shelf above the desk she brought out a toy animal, a dog maybe, and two dumb toy cars. At least my little brothers could be happy.

Captain Mindy went back to the shelf and I shook my head. I didn't want any more of their useless trinkets. She returned and held out a blue notebook with a metal spring binding and two new pens.

"*Baksheesh*," she said.

I had to dab at my eyes with my chador. A few days ago, I would have been thrilled by such a gift and the way the pen and paper would help me with Muallem's lessons. But what was the use of all that ancient poetry when I was doomed to be the same old Donkeyface? Donkeyface. I wiped the tears away and accepted the presents, putting all of my gifts into a plastic bag that the captain held open for me.

Baba gently pushed my shoulder. I finally looked up. "Tashakor."

Captain Mindy smiled but nervously turned a ring on her finger as she spoke.

"She is very sorry you won't be able to make it back here in a week for the flight. If you change your mind, she is sure we can still make this plan happen sometime," Shiaraqa said.

"We need to go," Baba said. "I have work."

Outside the building, I kept my chador tight over my ugly mouth. The captain crouched down in front of me again. Suddenly, she put her arms around me and there was nothing I could do but wait until this strange woman let me go.

Finally, Baba took hold of my arm and pulled me away. Captain Mindy stood up and smiled at my father, though something in her eyes had changed. She reached out her hand for him to shake. "*Tashakor*," she said. Baba ignored her and pulled me away.

And with a plastic bag full of toys, my notebook, and two pens, we were taken back to the front of the compound, where there was a new set of American soldiers guarding the gate. Again, these soldiers made a big fuss. Again, they insisted on shaking my hand. Then they put candy into my bag before Baba-jan and I were finally released and allowed to leave.

The inside of the car felt as hot as Malehkah's stove. I rolled down the window, sat back in the seat, and dropped my shawl. Baba got into the driver's seat and started the car, wiping the sweat from his forehead. He punched the steering wheel in front of him.

I gripped the top of my plastic bag in both hands and waited. Finally, Baba turned to me, took a deep breath, and let it out slowly. "That stupid American woman. You don't need their precious surgery. You're my daughter. You're pretty enough just as you are." That was it, then. He had decided. I would never be normal. "I am a very busy man, you know. Too busy to be worrying myself with this big complicated plan the Americans dreamed up."

I looked down at my hands, twisting the bag in my lap. It would be wrong to let my father see my disappointment after all he had been through today. Then I felt his big strong hand on my shoulder. He squeezed it and gave me a shake. When I looked up, he forced a smile. "Come on. Let's head back."

I turned away from my father and looked out the window, fingering my disgusting mouth as we passed the mounds of garbage on our way back home.

12

At supper, I still had to tilt my head back when I ate, pushing the rice deep in my mouth with my fingers to keep the food from slipping out. Even then, a few grains ended up in my lap. This was how I had always had to eat. I never thought about it as much as I did that night.

"Najibullah." My father ripped off a big piece of the beef and put it all in his mouth at once, wiping the spiced sauce from his lips with the back of his hand. When my brother didn't answer, Baba leaned over and lightly elbowed him as though Najib couldn't hear, even though they sat close. "We'll go out again tonight. I want to tack up those three support braces for tomorrow." He was a little hard to understand when he talked with food in his mouth.

I watched Zeynab beside me. She rolled the rice into a ball in her slender, graceful fingers and popped it into her perfect mouth without dropping a single grain. She must have noticed me watching her, because she smiled sadly.

My cheeks were hot with embarrassment. How could I allow myself to feel jealousy toward my sister, who had never been anything but completely kind to me? Envy was a sin and I prayed for forgiveness. I knew she had been excited, thinking about how wonderful everything leading up to her wedding would be. Our remaining time together was so short, and now I felt bad for ruining it. It was because of my stupid mouth that Baba had to waste a trip all the way to Farah. It was because of me that he was in such a terrible mood. If only that woman hadn't been so insulting. If only Baba could have been more patient and willing to work out some way I could still have the surgery.

I put my head back for another bite. After I had wiped my fingers on the cloth I always kept for meals, I saw Baba watching me. I thought he was going to say something to me, but instead he turned to Malehkah. "My brother and his family will be here next week. They're used to their fancy city apartment, so we'll let them have the storage room all to themselves. I want everything spotless. They think they're so much better than us. I don't want to let them think we live like slobs."

"I still think we're rushing. What will people think?" Malehkah said. "We already agreed to the marriage in only one meeting, and then the shirnee-khoree so soon after that, and now a wedding only two weeks after that? People will talk. They'll say we were too eager to get rid of Zeynab."

"Let them talk!" Baba spoke loudly. "What will they say? Hmm? Our darling girl will be marrying a sharp businessman. We'll be united by marriage and business to one of the richest, most honorable, most important families in An Daral."

Najib spoke quietly. "The Americans want the Nimruz Province clinic completed even earlier than we thought. The Abdullahs are going to help Baba-jan win the construction contract."

Baba grinned. "Tahir is a great man. He's making a lot of money in the trucking business, shipping food and supplies around Afghanistan for the Americans. Now he's expanding into making cement blocks. Since peace has come, everybody's building. He's going to cut us in on a percentage of his construction profits after we make him a couple of cement block handpress machines. All this would be a very generous bride-price, but he's also raised the amount of money to one hundred thousand Afghanis."

Malehkah nodded.

"Who needs all that old-fashioned stuff? Times are changing fast. If we want to keep up, we need to change too."

"It's tradition," said Malehkah.

Baba shook his head. "Old customs for an old Afghanistan. Still, I want the shahba-henna the night before the wedding to be just right. All the best food. Everything will be perfect for my sweet girl."

"If we could just hold off until—"

"Just do it!" Baba cut her off. "I get enough disrespect from that American woman. I won't have it in my own house." He groaned and braced himself on Najib's shoulder as he stood up.

"Bale," said Malehkah. She sighed quietly and looked across the table at Zeynab and me. "We'll be ready."

Khalid and Habib followed Baba and Najib outside to watch them load tools into the Toyota. Malehkah, Zeynab, and I sat around the little remaining food, staring at the mess that none of us wanted to clean.

✰ ✰ ✰

After the evening prayer, everyone slept but me.

154

I closed my eyes and tried to sleep, but behind my eyelids I kept seeing flashes of color that reminded me of the glints of sunlight on the steel teeth of the razor wire at the American base.

How could everything have gone so wrong? Worse, how could Baba act so casual about it all? It was as though he had almost completely forgotten about my surgery hopes already, and he barely seemed to notice that Zeynab was right there in the room as he discussed her wedding. He just went on with his business, all grumpy, making Malehkah, of all people, seem like the nice one.

It would have been better if the Americans had never even come to An Daral. I remembered them at the construction site with all their big guns. Their stupid guns and their stupid wars. All the dumb soldiers always ruining everything. Afghanistan had had too much of all of it.

My mother certainly had.

The beginning of my last memory of my mother was faded and vague now, but the end was always sharp and painful. Usually, I blocked it out and thought about something else, but sometimes I couldn't help but think of that night.

It was during the Taliban time. I had been sitting

on Madar-jan's lap in the center room of our house. She closed her big brown book, but I wanted her to read more. She laughed and recited some of the words from memory.

"Love fills the soul with sweetest tears,
The saddest songs one ever hears.
Flee deserts of heartless pain
With love that nourishes like rain."

Madar-jan wrapped her arms around me. "Your big sister always falls asleep, but you, little one, you love the poetry so much." I felt proud at that moment, like I was better than my pretty sister in at least one thing.

Zeynab was asleep next to Malehkah. I wouldn't have wanted Baba's new wife to sleep on my toshak, but since Malehkah hardly ever talked, she didn't say Zeynab couldn't sleep on hers.

"I love you. Promise me, my sweet princess. Promise me you'll read and learn all you can." Madar kissed the top of my head. "Even if the Taliban or somebody else tells you not to."

"Bale, Madar-jan," I said. "I promise."

"But for now you must go to sleep."

"It's too early to sleep. Too hot," I said. "Can't I wait for Baba and Najib?"

Madar shook her head. "They may be welding very late. Even I won't stay up for them. It's time for you and Zeynab to go up and go to sleep like baby Khalid."

Suddenly, there was an urgent knock on the door. Madar jumped, her eyes wide. Malehkah sat up and frowned at her.

"Malehkah, check the door." Madar dumped me from her lap and made for the storage room with her book. "I have to hide this."

Then a screeching metal crash came from outside. Madar froze. She turned and pulled Zeynab to her feet. "Take the kids to the roof. Try to keep them all quiet." Madar pushed Zeynab to Malehkah. Then she handed over the book. "And take this too."

"Saima, what —"

"Now, Malehkah!" my mother shouted.

Malehkah gripped Zeynab's wrist and hurried toward the stairs, pushing me the best she could while holding the book under her other arm. But I twisted around and got away. She carried my screaming sister up to the roof without me.

The front door of our house burst open, tearing off

its hinges. Baba was thrown into the room. He rolled across the floor and hit the wall with a groan. His eyes were swollen, and blood streamed down his beard from his mouth and nose. I screamed.

"Zulaikha, get upstairs!" Madar shrieked.

Three men in black turbans and very long beards stepped into the main room of our house. They were all holding guns. One of them took three quick steps toward my father and kicked him in the stomach.

"Please," Baba said. "Please, no more. In the trunk." He pointed toward the storage room. "They're in the trunk. I promise, that's all that's here. The only books she has."

"Sadiq, no!" Madar shouted. Her back was against the wall near the door to our small kitchen.

The man who must have been their leader nodded to his men. They went to our side storage room. I heard crashes, dishes breaking and trunks being thrown around. They came back, one of them holding two of my mother's books in his shaking hands.

"Oh, Sadiq." Tears rolled down my mother's face.

The leader strode up to my mother and swung his rifle like a club. I heard it crack against her jaw. Her blood splattered the wall.

"No, no, no, no, no!" Baba shouted. "You said you'd just take the—" The third man's boot crashed into my father's stomach once more.

Madar-jan spit white bits of teeth in a stream of red blood. The leader swung the rifle again. She raised her hands to protect her face, and her arm snapped like a dry stick as the rifle crashed into it. She screamed and dropped to her knees.

The leader pointed to the man with the books and then to the floor. The Talib dropped the books, pages flapping open. The leader took a bottle from his pocket and squirted something smelly onto the paper. He didn't take his eyes off my mother as he struck a match, holding the flame up before his face. He smiled. Then he dropped the match. The books puffed into flames, the pages curling back into black char. He spun around and kicked at my mother. His boot crunched into her chest and knocked her back against the wall.

"No! Please!" Baba cried.

The leader snapped at his men, who stomped on my bloodied father to hold him down.

"Go away!" I shouted, my fists clenched tight.

The big man turned to face me. His eyes were squinted and lined in black. But when he took a step

159

toward me, my mother was on her feet, pushing out her good arm to stop him.

He grabbed her by the hair. Madar screamed as he pulled her out the door to the front courtyard. The other two held my struggling father to the floor.

There was screaming. Shouting. Screaming.

A shot like thunder.

After the men had left, there was only crying. I went to the door. My father knelt in the dust, wailing over my mother in the courtyard.

"Saima, my Saima, I'm so sorry. Saima."

✷ ✷ ✷

Years later, lying on my toshak, surrounded by my sleeping family, I thought of my lost madar-jan and my lost opportunity for the surgery that would make me look pretty. All my chances for happiness had been stolen away. I buried my face in my chador and cried.

13

A week later, the sun burned hotter than it had all summer. The Winds of 120 Days gusted full upon us, but did nothing to cool us down. Sweat ran down my face. It tasted like tears when it ran into my mouth through the gap in my upper lip. After a day of cooking and cleaning to make sure all was prepared for the shahba-henna tonight, Malehkah had decided it was time for Zeynab to rest while she sent me to the construction site with food for Baba, Najib, and Uncle Ghobad, who had arrived that morning with his wife and Malehkah's mother. The men had met at Hajji Abdullah's house the night before to officially settle the bride-price, so they planned to just keep on working until well after dark.

I walked down the street in the blazing heat with the bundle of naan held awkwardly under my arm. The wire handle from the heavy pot of rice dug into my hand. The road in this section of town was even more rough and uneven than other roads, and so

I had to watch the ground to avoid tripping. I should have been paying more attention to my surroundings. A shadow approached, and I looked up to see Anwar blocking my path. He stood with his arms folded over his chest and smiled in a cruel way. He leaned in and squinted his eyes to take a good look at my mouth.

"Hmm. Nope," he said. "Still ugly old Donkeyface. Not even the rich Americans with their fancy machines and doctors could fix that mangled mouth and nose of yours." I tried to step around him, but he moved to keep standing in my way. "Whoa there, Donkeyface! What's your hurry?"

"Can you please just let me pass, Anwar? I need to get this food to my father."

Anwar pretended like he was about to vomit. "Ugh, don't say my name. You sound as ugly as you look when you talk."

"I'll just yell for help. We're close enough. My baba will hear."

Anwar laughed. "I don't think your father would want you shouting all over town like some whore. Besides, he'd be angry if he knew you were causing me trouble. Without my father's help and the bride-price my uncle paid to marry your sister, *your* father would be as pathetic and poor as he ever was!"

I couldn't stand listening to him for another moment. I swung the pot of rice at his knees. When he jumped back out of the way, I ran past him. He did not follow, but I could hear him laughing behind me.

"Khuda hafiz, Donkeyface! I'll see you at the wedding!"

I slowed down as I approached the school site, marveling at how quickly the building had grown. Baba had said the welding was almost complete. On top of a big cement platform was a giant cage of steel beams and poles. Baba was welding at the base of one of them.

"Don't look at the light, Zulaikha," said Najib, walking toward me. I turned away from the shower of sparks that fell from where Baba worked. Najib took the covered pot of rice and the wrapped naan out of my hands, setting them on a low mudstone wall. He patted his skinny stomach over his sweat-soaked perahan-tunban. "I'm hungry."

Baba finished making his white sparks on the steel pipes he was joining. He took off his heavy mask, turned down dials on two different tanks, and then flipped a switch on a machine. After that, he walked over to take a seat on the wall. "Tashakor, Zulaikha." His hair was wet and his shirt was so soaked with sweat that it looked like he'd taken a dip in an irrigation canal. He wiped at his forehead, letting his hands run slowly down his face. When his fingertips sank below his eyes, he looked at me. "My brother get here yet?"

I shook my head. Uncle Ramin's family was supposed to be on a bus from Kabul to Farah. We were expecting their taxi from Farah at any time. Malehkah and her mother and sister had been grumbling all morning, accusing them of being late on purpose to get out of helping with the shahba-henna.

"Are you staying to eat with us?" Uncle Ghobad asked. He had said he was going to the construction site to help Baba and Najib, but he was a carpenter, and by the look of how clean he was, it didn't seem like he had worked very much.

I shrugged. "Madar wants me to buy some things for tonight at the bazaar."

Baba dropped one hand to his lap and rubbed the back of his neck with the other. "She sends you out a lot, doesn't she?" Somehow I didn't think he wanted an answer. He continued. "More than she used to anyway. After she has the baby, she should start going herself. It's not good for a young unmarried girl to be running all over town."

164

Why was it not good? Baba couldn't seriously be worried about some boy trying to touch or kiss me. The only boys who chased me called me mean names or threw rocks.

"Bale, Baba," I said.

"Okay," he said. "Hurry home. Your madar and sister will need your help to get ready for tonight." He turned his attention to a piece of naan.

With a nod to my brother, I turned and walked off to the bazaar, where I bought Malehkah the peppers she claimed she needed, though I was sure I saw some in the kitchen just last night.

"I don't suppose I could solicit your help in carrying these bolts of fabric?" The voice came from a pile of cloth, tottering at the side of the road as I went through the butcher district. Meena. I sighed and took off the top three rolls of cloth, uncovering a smiling face that looked the opposite of what I felt. "Salaam alaikum!"

"Walaikum salaam," I greeted the old teacher, and we walked out of the bazaar together. Today I'd really make Malehkah wait. Why not? She always said I took too long at the bazaar even when I hurried.

"How has the writing practice gone?" Meena asked, once we were back at her apartment and had stowed away the fabric. She had poured me a cup of tea. "Have you been copying the words?"

I nodded, but said nothing. How could she be asking about her dreamy poetry when it was obvious that my dream of finally looking normal was a failure? Why did she not ask why I was still so ugly? My big, split-open mouth was right in front of her.

The silence was uncomfortable. I thought about leaving, but Meena always trapped me with tea. I would have to stay at least as long as it took to finish my cup.

"Zulaikha?" Meena asked. I couldn't answer her. "What is the matter? Is it the surgery?" Of course it was the surgery! How could she be so blind and still be able to read? "The Americans were not able to help you. I'm sorry, child."

I sipped my tea, hating myself for having to tilt my head back so that I could drink. More quiet.

"Do you want to show me how you've improved your writing?"

"No," I said. And right then I knew what I wanted to say to her. "I won't be studying any more." I pointed to my mouth. "What difference does it make to a girl like me? Reading won't fix my mouth. Poetry won't find me a husband. It's all just a bunch of useless old words in dusty old books." I stood up. "I'm sorry. I have to go."

Meena put her cup down on the table, and lowered her hands and her gaze to her lap. "It's a pity."

I nodded. "I just should never have even thought it was possible for my mouth to be fixed."

"No, child. The pity is that you're placing so much importance on the temporary. On physical appearance. Beauty. These things fade in time, but the literature that your mother loved – that you love – is timeless." Meena watched me with deep, dark eyes.

I wished she could somehow understand. "I'm not as smart as my madar. Not as pretty." There was a stinging in my eyes. I wanted to leave before the tears began to fall. "Your books. They aren't my life." I wiped my eyes. "I need to get home." I started for the front door.

"Why did you want the surgery?"

I stopped and took a deep breath. "I already told you. I want to look normal."

"And if you looked, as you say, 'normal,' what would you do then?"

I turned around and faced her. "What?"

Meena slid back across her bed so she could lean against the wall. "If you had your surgery and looked normal, what would you do?" I was about to answer but she interrupted. "Would you get married like your sister? Then what?"

"What do you mean, then what?" I folded my arms across my chest. What kind of stupid questions were these? "People wouldn't be disgusted at the sight of me!"

Meena shook her head. "You'd have a husband who wasn't disgusted by your appearance."

"Yes!" I threw my arms out wide.

"And how would your life be different then than it is now?"

"I don't know! It would be – I mean, I wouldn't always have to listen to..." She couldn't expect me to want to stay looking like this, could she? She couldn't expect me to be happy that I couldn't have the surgery. "It would be different because I wouldn't waste my time with your stupid old books!"

I stormed through the sewing shop and out the door into the street. I wasn't about to stay around and listen to more of Meena's crazy talk. My sister and Malehkah needed help getting ready for Zeynab's party, and I wasn't going to let them down. It was time to stop these selfish dreams. It was time to get back to what really mattered.

Zeynab was sitting on the porch when I came into the compound. She was trying to cool herself with a fan I'd made her from some of the notebook paper the Americans had given me. She wore her pretty pink and purple flowered dress, and blew out an exhausted breath through lips red with lipstick. "Oh, why do we have to do this at the hottest time of year?" She tried to laugh, but she was unconvincing. I shared in her misery. It was nearly sundown, her last night with us, and still the heat blazed and the sand and grit flew on the wind.

Malehkah came out of the house. "Into the sitting room, both of you." She hurried us across the courtyard and into the little room where her mother and sister were already waiting. She took the peppers from me, slipping them into her pockets. Then she pushed a wet rag in my face. "Wash up the best you can." She rushed around, straightening the cushions.

"But Madar, it's an oven in here," said Zeynab.

"Then that's the way it will be," said Farida. "But if you don't stay inside, your makeup will be full of dust."

"Then what will your new family think of you?" said Tayereh.

The only thing worse than listening to Malehkah

yell at us was having her mother and sister around to yell at us even more. Malehkah groaned as she lowered herself to the floor and leaned back against a toshak. "The food is ready. We can all rest for a few minutes."

Zeynab slumped on the small couch that Hajji Abdullah had brought over again. The sitting room was as clean as it was going to get in these winds, with wet rags stuffed at the base of the door to keep out the dust. Outside, the wind howled. Then over the sound of the wind came the even louder sound of one of the boys crying. After taking Habib and Khalid with him to Hajji Abdullah's house for the men's shirnee-khoree, Baba had decided the boys were too much trouble to have at the men's parties. Tonight, when the women came over for the shahba-henna, we'd have to look after the little ones.

"Zulaikha, go check on them. Then bring in the pistachios." Malehkah sighed and handed me the peppers I had bought. Then she wiped her brow and rubbed her swollen ankles.

"Bale, Madar."

In the house, the boys were sitting on the floor in the main room, their toy soldiers spread out all over. I had tried to keep them busy and moving around all day so that they'd be exhausted and sleep through the party. Now they were arguing over who could play with which men. I didn't waste time trying to reason with them. From my trunk in the side room, I brought out one of the only good things to come from my wasted trip to Farah. "Here, Khalid." I handed him one of the metal toy cars. His eyes went wide.

"This is great! It's real metal just like Baba's car!" Khalid put the car on the floor and pushed it around. His lips buzzed, making an engine sound.

"You're welcome," I whispered.

Habib's lower lip trembled, but before he started crying again, I handed him his own car. He smiled big at me and then imitated his brother. I had known it would be a good idea to wait to give them some of their presents.

"You handled that well." Zeynab had followed me into the house.

"It's too hot for you to be running all over the compound. You'll ruin your makeup," I called as I entered the kitchen. "Anyway, I think I can find the pistachios by myself."

When I returned to the main room with the bowl of nuts, Zeynab hugged me. "Thank you for being so nice and helping with all of this. I…"

171

She fanned her face.

I squeezed Zeynab close. "You're my sister. I'd do anything for you."

She took my hands in hers. "I can't believe tonight will be my last night here at home. I'll miss you so much," she said. "I promise you can visit my new house all the time. Farah isn't really that far away. Baba has the car now. Tahir often comes to An Daral to visit his brother, so he'll bring me here... and... and hey, you'll be able to get away from Malehkah sometimes when you come to see me. I know that—"

"Girls! Get out here!" Malehkah's shrill call came from outside.

"I love you," I whispered in Zeynab's ear.

We went out of the house hand in hand. From the sound of all the voices coming from inside the sitting room, it was clear that the guests had arrived. They must have all showed up at the same time. When we entered, the sitting room was a whirlwind of chadris and the enthusiastic greetings of excited women. Gulzoma, Jamila, Isma, and the other women of the Abdullah family were there, but they had been joined by Aunt Halima and her daughter Khatira.

"Zeynab! Zulaikha! Look at you! Oh, you've grown up so fast!" Aunt Halima hugged both of us in turn.

Our cousin Khatira was next. She hugged my sister. "It's great to see you again! I'm so happy that long trip is finally over!" Then she put her arms around me stiffly before holding me back at arm's length and frowning at my mouth. "Ooh, that's too bad. I'd heard that the Americans had offered you surgery to fix your lip." She pouted. "If only these rural villages had the kind of hospitals that we have in Kabul, I'm sure—"

"Come along, Khatira," said Aunt Halima.

My cousin nodded. "Bale, Madar-jan."

"Yes!" Gulzoma spoke loudly so that everyone had to listen. "It is just too bad Zulaikha couldn't get the surgery. You never can tell with those Americans. They promise to fix up all of Afghanistan and get rid of the Taliban completely. Then they get here and find out it isn't so easy." She peered closely at my lip. "I bet they just realized that your mouth was too deformed for even their fancy doctors to fix."

"I'm sure that wasn't the case," said Aunt Halima.

"We'll never know," Gulzoma answered.

It was happening all over again. The humiliation. The polite-sounding insults. It was bad enough to hear the hurtful words, but I just wished the party could go smoothly tonight for Zeynab's sake. I was relieved when Malehkah and Gulzoma began making many introductions and everyone sat down, just like the night of the engagement party. "We're sorry, Zeynab," Jamila said. "I know everyone was probably expecting dancing tonight, but my brother's wife and I are getting too old for all that pre-wedding dancing bit." She leaned back next to Gulzoma. "Besides, there will be plenty of dancing after everybody has cake at the arusi."

Gulzoma elbowed Jamila, nodded toward Zeynab, and spoke out, "But you might want to save your energy for the wedding night."

All the women laughed at the vulgar joke, except my sister, who only forced a smile.

For once I welcomed Malehkah's demands when she told me to go with her to the house and start bringing in the meal. After everyone had washed and begun eating, the conversation began to flow as it had at the shirnee-khoree. Gulzoma had even more stories, but the Abdullah women were also full of questions about Kabul. Aunt Halima seemed happy to answer. The night went on for hours. Eventually I was sent to check on my sleeping brothers and to bring in a tray of sweet cakes and fruit.

I returned to the sitting room amid the sound of laughter. Gulzoma continued with a story that she told in a very lively way, clapping her hands and almost rolling about where she was sitting. "Well, the tables had turned, you see. American jets swooped over the skies, bombing everything." She swooshed her hand around like a plane, the palm wide open. "The Taliban were on the run. And would you believe it, but this same little man, this boy Talib came crawling back to my husband asking for a job?" She burst into a deep bellowing laugh that shook her whole body. The other women were shaking their heads. "… No… no, it's true," she said through her laughter. "He asked my husband to give him a job working to help build the American compound at Farah! Oh, good. Bananas!"

I placed the tray on the dastarkhan, then took a cake to Zeynab. As the other women had stopped listening so they could pick out their treats, Gulzoma frowned, peeling the banana she'd taken with exaggerated movements.

"What did Hajji Abdullah tell him?" asked Farida when everyone had something.

Gulzoma threw her hands up in the air, flopping the banana peel all around. "Now you will think my husband told that little Talib to go eat sand.

But he's much smarter than that. My husband gave the man a job serving food to the other workers at lunch time." She paused and looked around the room with her hands in her lap. Then she burst out, "Then he reported the Talib to the Americans, who brought him in for questioning!"

"Wah wah! Gulzoma!" Jamila shouted.

The big lady's smile seemed genuine at last as she looked around the room, enjoying the cheers, clapping, and laughter. "When the Americans came for him, he was shaking, almost crying."

"A man crying, grandmother?" said a small girl.

"The Taliban were not men." Gulzoma leaned forward as her voice became quiet. "My husband says he never saw the Talib again."

"So my brother Hajji Abdullah is a hero," Jamila said.

I never liked Taliban talk. I smoothed out the dastarkhan and straightened some of the dishes.

"What's the matter, Zulaikha? Don't you like the story?" Gulzoma said.

Malehkah was smiling, but her eyes were somehow still hard, still cold. I had to say the exact right thing. I looked at my sister, who twisted her dress tight in her lap.

"He and his brother Tahir have talked to the Americans for my father about my surgery." I was surprised that I had spoken out loud. I risked a glance at Malehkah, who glared at me. I squeezed my hands into tight fists.

Everyone was quiet again and Gulzoma stared at me. "What did you say, Zulaikha?"

I swallowed and covered my mouth. I had to keep going. "Jamila-jan said that Hajji Abdullah is a hero. I was agreeing because I am very grateful for his help with the Americans. Their helicopter couldn't come to Farah, and with the wedding, there was no time to take the trip to their doctor in Kandahar. But if they almost" – I waved my hand in front of my mouth – "fixed this, Hajji Abdullah is as much to thank as the Americans." Nobody spoke. They all just kept looking at me. I must have said too much. I blinked my eyes, trying to stop the hot tears of embarrassment from falling. "Please thank him for me." I lowered my head as the first tear fell.

"Look at the poor dear. She can hardly talk with that mouth. She hasn't even been fixed and she's so grateful to my husband that she's crying with gratitude. Oooh." Gulzoma clapped her hands, and when I looked up she was beckoning for me to come closer. "Come here and sit by your Gulzoma-jan."

As much as I hated the idea of being close to Gulzoma, and as embarrassed as I felt for my big dumb speech, I wasn't stupid enough to disobey her. I stood up and walked around the circle of women to take a place beside her. She slipped a heavy damp arm around my shoulder and pulled me in to lean against her.

"You sweet little angel." She looked up from me to Malehkah. "My husband is such a good man by nature that he often hardly realizes how much he has helped people." Gulzoma turned to one of the women whose name I had forgotten. "You brought that tambourine, didn't you?" The woman nodded. "Then let's make some music! I feel so close to this family already that we just have to dance. Sometimes you can't help yourself, even if you are full to bursting on such delightful food." She pulled me against her heavily perfumed body as everyone started singing, laughing, and dancing.

I looked to Malehkah. She gently nodded her approval. Then her sister elbowed her and laughed. Malehkah turned her attention toward the music, clapping her hands along with the beat of the tambourine. She didn't seem angry with me for all

I had said. That was a relief, but the best part was that my sister's party had been rescued from dreary awkwardness.

Women jiggled around like I'd never seen anyone move. They laughed and shook their bodies and even pinched and slapped each other in private places. Gulzoma didn't dance, but she shook around with the rhythm and sometimes joined in singing the songs. She kept me by her side. Being so close to her, and being packed into a small room in the middle of summer with all those frantic dancing women, made the room very hot.

The party continued as one by one, each married woman made her way through the chaos to sit on the little couch beside Zeynab. I couldn't hear what they were saying, but I knew they were giving her advice about being a wife. This advice must have been the reason Malehkah had insisted on Zeynab wearing so much makeup – to hide her embarrassed blushing at what she heard.

As soon as one song ended, another began. Once, Gulzoma shook me. "Oh, Zulaikha! You must dance for us!"

I looked at her with surprise. "I don't know how. I've never—"

"Ah, you silly little thing!" Gulzoma laughed. "We all learn some time."

Malehkah coughed and nodded toward the space before Zeynab. I stood up. All night I'd watched how smoothly the women danced. They all seemed to know the perfect movements for each song. Some of the women hooted as the music rolled on. At first, I thought they were mocking me, but their smiles seemed sincere. I threw my arm up and out from my side, then spun away, trailing my other arm in an arc over my face. Almost on its own, my foot flew forward and I pointed my toe on the floor. I swayed from side to side with my toe pointed out and my hands above my head.

Was I doing it right? I didn't know. Somehow I didn't care. The singing and clapping took over in the heat. The music and dancing held a power very much like Meena's poetry, its rhythm calling out to me from across time. Someone had danced before my madar-jan's wedding. Before the Taliban had outlawed music, she had probably danced as well. The song ended, and although Zeynab wasn't supposed to show emotion, I saw the happy glimmer of tears in her eyes.

Finally, when it was very late, Malehkah spoke up.

"It is time for the henna." And so, while she held a dish of mint-green-colored paste, and with a lot of advice from the other women, I painted swirls and flowers all over Zeynab's hands and feet, trying my best to make my designs as delicate as I could.

"It tickles." She giggled. Then she dropped her voice to the quietest whisper. "Thank you for helping to make this night so wonderful."

I nodded and touched her shoulder.

When I finished painting the paste on my sister's hands and feet, I wrapped them in a glittery scarf that we'd been saving just for tonight. Later, after the Abdullahs had said good night and gone home, I helped Zeynab lie down on a mat with a pillow under her head, and we all settled down to sleep. As I rested close to my sister, the reality set in. This was our last night together. Tomorrow, she would belong to her new husband.

That thought must have occurred to my sister as well, for soon she shook with tiny sobs. I stroked her hair. In this way, we drifted off to sleep, together.

14

The next morning before prayers, Malehkah and I washed off the dried henna to reveal the deep amber and brown swirls on Zeynab's skin. It looked beautiful, but we couldn't admire it for long. There was a large breakfast to cook after prayers. Baba didn't want to give Uncle Ramin a chance to complain about the food.

After that, most of the hot day was devoted to getting ready for the nikah. We cleaned both the house and the people in it. I swept and scrubbed the sitting room on my own while Malehkah and Zeynab bathed Khalid and Habib. Later, when the sitting room and house were ready and all of us were washed and dressed in our best, it was time to prepare Zeynab.

In the side storage room, I helped my sister into the beautiful embroidered green dress that she and I had worked on and dreamed about for years. "Are you nervous?" I straightened the back of her dress.

"Hmm. I think maybe there are two kinds of

nervous." Zeynab closed her eyes as I brushed thick white makeup onto her cheeks. "There's that feeling you get when you are worried about doing something you don't want to do. Then there's a happy anxious feeling, when you're excited because a wonderful and important moment is approaching. I'm happy nervous."

"I'm happy too," I said. Neither of us spoke as I finished putting on her makeup and curled her hair, pinning it up into a pretty crown. Maybe I should have said more, but we'd been so close for so long that we didn't always need to talk, especially when all that remained to discuss was what we both already knew. This was the end of our time together, and although we'd always dreamed about our weddings, now that Zeynab's had come, we would miss each other terribly.

The door opened. Malehkah and all the other women came in. She examined Zeynab and nodded. "Tahir is in the sitting room with the rest of the men. The mullah has arrived."

Zeynab squeezed my hand and stepped toward the door. "Should we go?"

"Just wait." Malehkah held up her hand. "The mullah will send two witnesses to ask if you are willing to get married. After they take back your answer, your father will sign the papers for you. Then the mullah will lead a prayer and the nikah will be over."

"You mean, they don't even need her to be there?" Khatira asked.

Malehkah's mother and sister laughed. Aunt Halima hugged her daughter. Malehkah scowled. "I wasn't present for mine." She shrugged. "It's tradition." Zeynab frowned. When Malehkah saw her disappointed look, she went on.

"There'll be plenty to do at the arusi in Hajji Abdullah's house. Gulzoma says she's even hired two bands, one for the men and one for the women's party." She sighed. "Should be quite a show."

Then it was quiet for a while. We waited, and I held Zeynab's hand.

After a few minutes, Najib and Baba's brother Ramin came to the door and asked Zeynab if she was willing to marry Tahir. Of course she said yes. Then they left and we waited some more. I squeezed my sister's hand. It was really happening. The long-awaited wedding day had finally arrived. These were her last few minutes living here at home.

"Malehkah?" Baba's voice came from just outside

the door. His happiness seemed to charge his every word. "It's time to go!" When Malehkah opened the door, he stepped in, wearing his new Western-style suit. She shook her head. "Don't be so grumpy," he said to her. "This suit was a much better idea than any old perahan-tunban. Tahir is a smart businessman. He's invited the Americans to the wedding." He smoothed his hand down over the silly strip of cloth that hung down from his neck, this thing he called a *tie*. "Rude as they are, they probably won't bother to show up. But if they do, I'll be ready to show them that I'm just the man for all their welding needs. HA!" He clapped his hands. "But that's enough complicated men's talk. Zeynab, your husband's family is outside and ready to take you to Hajji Abdullah's for the arusi." He went back out to the sitting room.

I regretted not saying anything while we waited through the nikah. Now I wanted to tell Zeynab so much, but everything was happening very fast.

After a few minutes, we could hear the singing – happy songs of love and hope. Malehkah and I helped Zeynab into her chadri and led her out of the house to the front courtyard, where most of the women who had been at the shahba-henna awaited her. Just before they took her outside to the street where their cars waited, Zeynab squeezed my hand.

The arusi was usually held at the groom's home, but since Tahir lived over an hour away in Farah, Hajji Abdullah had offered the use of his beautiful new house for the occasion. Uncle Ramin rode up front in Baba's Toyota. Najib, Halima, Khatira, and I rode in the back seat. Uncle Ghobad, Malehkah, her family, and the boys followed in their car.

As we approached the Abdullah compound in the new section of town, Baba smiled and pointed. "You see? Look. Look at that compound. No mud-brick walls there. No. All cement block. Look at all those colored tiles on the second floor. He's got a big porch up there where you can see down into his back courtyard and out to the mountains. And all of this built just in the last year since he's been working for the Americans!"

"And now you're building for the Americans too, Uncle Sadiq," said Khatira.

Baba's grin was hard not to catch. "Yes. And my darling daughter is marrying a great man today." He tooted the horn and smiled.

Baba parked our Toyota just off the dirt road in front of the Abdullah compound. We tumbled out of the vehicle. I smoothed out my freshly cleaned pink

Eid dress the best I could. We went up the path past many cars. The sound of music came from inside the compound. Zeynab must have already gone in. Habib stopped for a moment and looked up with an open mouth at the big house, but Khalid grabbed him by the wrist and pulled him along. When we reached the compound gate, Baba knocked on a colorful door, but I was not prepared for what I saw when the door opened.

"Salaam. Welcome to our home." Anwar. He spoke with his right hand over his heart as he bowed to the men. On his face was a grin like the one he had whenever he'd just pulled off a particularly cruel stunt. His eyes quickly swept us all, stopping for just the smallest instant on me. I pulled my chador up to cover my mouth as Anwar stepped back and motioned for us to pass him and go inside. "Please come in."

Everyone went through the gate, and Anwar made a little bow to Baba again. "If you will follow me? The men are celebrating inside where it is cool. The women can head down this hall to the back courtyard."

Baba-jan thanked Anwar, who led him down a separate corridor. Baba gently pushed Uncle Ramin, Uncle Ghobad, and Najib ahead while he held back a moment. He held out his hands to Khalid and Habib and spoke louder so the little boys would be sure to listen. "Let's see if you're big enough to behave yourselves at the men's party this time." Then he led my little brothers away to celebrate with the men.

"Come on." Malehkah beckoned with the veil she carried, leading us all down the hallway toward the back of the house. "I need to get out of this chadri and sit down. Besides, we don't want to keep the women waiting."

The Abdullah house was a massive two-story castle, easily four or five times the size of our little mud-brick home. The entire front courtyard was cement save for a circle cut out for a palm tree. Flowers grew in little pots everywhere. The back courtyard was much the same, except a larger part was left without cement for a garden. In the center of the back courtyard was a beautiful, circular fountain with colored tiles, a column of water spurting up in its center and streams of water arching from the outer ring toward the middle. Women were already seated on rugs, talking and drinking tea. Would Zeynab live in a house like this? If so, it was a good thing Tahir had two other wives. She would need a lot of help to keep such a large house clean.

"There you *are*!" Gulzoma came out of one of the back doors of the castle onto the stone porch.

She wore a flowing blue dress and spread her big arms out wide. "Come on, all of you, take those chadris off and come up here. Zeynab is waiting right inside. She looks absolutely beautiful." When the women had removed their chadris, Gulzoma swept up Malehkah in an embrace. "Malehkah, you look lovely. Such a pretty dress." She stepped back and put her hands on her hips. "Have you been sneaking visits to my tailor? Meena is so talented. She made this for me just for this wedding." Gulzoma spun around, showing off her blue dress. My face grew hot with the mention of sneaking visits to the tailor. Meena was more talented than Gulzoma would ever know.

Just when Malehkah was about to reply, Gulzoma switched her attention to her mother and sister. It was as if Malehkah had vanished and her family had suddenly appeared on a wind. "Farida! Tayereh!" She put heavy emphasis on each of their names as though it was the first time she'd ever heard them. "I can see good taste runs in the family!" She turned to look at Halima and Khatira and spread her fingers over her chest. "And are *those* the latest styles from Kabul? Beautiful!"

Then she ran her hands down the sleeves of my dress. "Oooh, my baby girl! My little bird. There just aren't words." I suspected that somehow Gulzoma would find more than a few words. She kissed my cheeks, one after the other, then pulled me to her, smothering me against her big chest. "Look at you, in a pretty dress. Trying to look pretty but with your poor, poor mouth." She was making such a big show of my mouth that other guests were starting to look. "Oooh!" She leaned forward and spoke quietly. "Don't you worry. I am going to convince my husband to make those Americans get you all fixed up." She spun me around to stand beside her with her arm draped over my shoulders. "She's a bird. Just a very bird! We are going to get her all fixed up. I just know it."

When she stopped to breathe, I thought it best to take my opportunity. "Tashakor, Gulzoma. I am very grateful."

"I'm sure you are! I'm just sure you are. You sweet little thing. You bird."

I really wished she would stop calling me 'bird'.

Gulzoma led us through a set of double glass doors into a beautiful room with a carpeted floor, a soft sofa, two chairs, and a small polished wooden table on which rested a tray of fruit and some bottles of water. Zeynab sat on the sofa, trying to hold back her smile. She looked at me and then at Gulzoma.

I was sure she had heard everything outside. "Here she is!" Gulzoma squeezed my sister's arm. "So beautiful! Here is where you will wait until it's time for you to walk up and join Tahir by our fountain. I have to go make sure the servants are taking care of the guests. Half the town of An Daral is going to be here." She laughed. "Our family is large, but my husband has also invited others, even the Americans. And though I begged him not to, he just *had* to invite the Farah Province governor!" She leaned toward Malehkah and lowered her voice as though telling a big secret. "I really hope he doesn't come. You know, I was just saying the other—"

"Gulzoma!" A stern voice boomed from another part of the house.

Gulzoma instantly stood straight up and turned serious. "My husband." She glided out of the room.

Zeynab let out a breath. "I'm glad she's gone." We snickered, but Malehkah turned a warning glare on us both.

"This is the home of your host. You will not disrespect anyone who lives here."

"Bale, Madar," we said together.

She leaned in close to us. "Do not embarrass your father," she warned. She turned to me so that her

191

face was inches from mine, the wrinkles around her eyes folding into deep creases as she scowled at me. "Remember your place, Zulaikha. Remember your duty."

"Bale, Madar."

Zeynab turned her head to the side. "Madar, why are you so upset? Why can't you be happy? This is supposed to be a happy day."

Malehkah snorted. "Your special day." Then her expression softened and her eyes glistened just a little. "Oh, Zeynab," she said.

My sister's mouth fell open and she looked at Malehkah, wide-eyed. "Madar? What is it?"

Malehkah shook her head and then forced a smile. "Nothing." She wiped her eyes. "Nothing. Let's just make this day the best it can be."

This apparently satisfied Zeynab. "Tashakor, Madar."

Malehkah only nodded. I couldn't get past the feeling that she had wanted to say more – that Zeynab had been too easily comforted by her false smile. I looked at my father's wife as she ate a banana from the tray. No matter what she said, she seemed determined to ruin Zeynab's dream wedding. I clenched my fists. I'd just have to work extra hard to make sure the day was perfect.

The sound of voices and laughter made me peek through the curtain covering the door to the back porch. Dozens of women were crowding the courtyard. The men must have been filling up other parts of the house. Children rushed around serving the women. I touched my split upper lip. My hand was sweaty. I forced myself to think about Zeynab and not about having to go out there in front of all those people.

At least it was as wonderful a setting as Zeynab and I had ever dreamed of. The servants were bringing out the food. It was a lot like last night's feast, but of course, here at the Abdullah house, there was more. I could see roast chicken, mutton, beef, and goat. Enormous bowls of rice with little pieces of carrots and raisins. Roasted buttered potatoes. Radishes, pickled cucumbers, and peppers. Bowls of nuts. Bowls of candies. Oranges, apples, bananas, and pomegranates. Almost all that An Daral had to offer for food, plus some things from the bazaar in Farah City, were laid out for the enjoyment of the guests.

Three women brought their musical instruments out and took seats on a rug off to the side of the fountain. One set up her tabla drums. Another began to warm up by squeezing her harmonium and pressing the keys. The third strummed and plucked the strings on her rubab, turning wooden keys at the top of its neck to adjust the sound. I looked back at Malehkah and my sister. "The women's band!" Not in our most elaborate fantasies had we ever dreamed that Zeynab could have a band just for the women's party at her wedding.

"It won't be long now," said Malehkah. "Soon, Tahir will come."

"Bale, Madar." Zeynab's voice was shaky.

We waited and waited, while out in the courtyard more and more women arrived. Finally, Malehkah snapped her fingers. "The veil. It's almost time."

I carefully helped her lift the veil over Zeynab's head. Now, in the beautiful green dress that she and I had worked on for years, with the soft white veil over her face and her hair curled up atop her head like a crown, my sister literally shone. The sequins on the skirt of her dress sparkled.

"You're beautiful," I said.

"So are you," she whimpered through tears.

"I love—"

"No! What are you doing? No crying! You'll make a mess of your makeup and your eyes will be all red." Malehkah took Zeynab's white wedding cloth from her pocket, pulled the veil back up, and dabbed carefully at her eyes. "You are not a child any more, Zeynab. You can't be crying like this. They'll think you don't want to get married. They'll think you're ungrateful. Imagine what they'll say about your father if you go out there with all these tears. You have responsibilities."

"But Madar, I—"

My father's wife cracked her hand across Zeynab's cheek.

Zeynab and I were silent and still. We stared at Malehkah in horror. Malehkah waited for a moment, her eyes wide, as though she was challenging us to defy her. Then she sighed, handed me the wedding cloth, pulled Zeynab's veil back down, and went back to the curtain. "Remember what I have told both of you."

We didn't answer. Malehkah may have shocked the tears out of my sister, but she had also taken the last bit of joy from the room. She turned around and looked us both over. "He's coming. Be ready."

Zeynab turned her eyes toward the floor. She was not supposed to look at her husband. It was especially wrong to make eye contact with him. She sighed.

"Shh. Quiet," Malehkah hissed.

I peeked around the curtain again. Finally, Tahir stood waiting in the front near the fountain. He was clean-shaven and his dark hair was flecked with just enough gray to make him handsome. Wrinkles in his forehead and at the corners of his eyes suggested wisdom and reminded me of Baba-jan. He wore a nice new embroidered perahan-tunban and several gold rings on his fingers. He was very tall.

"Oh, Zeynab," I said. "He's amazing. He looks so strong and sure."

Malehkah nodded and opened the doors. "It's time," she said, ushering Zeynab outside.

The music out in the courtyard changed to something slower and more somber, and Tahir smiled, looking down as well.

Zeynab and I had often dreamed of her wedding day, but never had we imagined her husband to be so much older. Older, maybe, than Baba-jan. Still, this was the way of things, right? Baba was much older than Malehkah. Besides, Baba-jan loved us all and was certain that he had found Zeynab the perfect husband. I looked again at the big man who waited for Zeynab. He was established and strong. A good Muslim, to be blessed with so much wealth.

"Be a good woman," Malehkah said quietly in

my ear. She handed me a cloth-wrapped Holy Quran. "Do not disappoint your father." She went out and sat down on a rug near the front. I held the Holy Book over my sister's head as I followed her slowly to the fountain.

Once Zeynab stood by Tahir's side, they played around at whose foot would be in front of the other person's. It was said that the foot that ended up in front belonged to the boss of the marriage. Zeynab finally lost, as was expected, and there were chuckles and murmurs from the women.

Then it was time for them to sit on their throne, the same small, red, cushioned couch that Hajji Abdullah had brought to our house for Zeynab last night. Now whoever was last to sit down would be the boss of the marriage. When Malehkah had told us all of these wedding rules, Zeynab and I had laughed, thinking these little rituals were cute. It was cute now, too, and I smiled behind my chador as Tahir and Zeynab each stood facing forward, neither one willing to sit down. Then Gulzoma came up to the front with her hands on her big hips and an amused frown on her face. She smiled at me and at all the women, then she put her hands on both Tahir and Zeynab's shoulders, gently pushing them both down at the same time until they sat. Everybody chuckled and clapped. Gulzoma bowed to everyone and returned to where she sat near Malehkah.

Now I knew it was my turn. I took a deep breath and carefully placed the Holy Quran on a small table near the couple. I pulled my chador over my mouth. My legs shook and my hands were sweaty as I felt so many eyes watching me. I was grateful, at least, that the men celebrated the wedding separately.

I felt a hand press my back and turned to see my cousin Khatira. She nodded at the green, lace-edged shawl on the table. Together we held up the shawl by all four corners over Zeynab and her new husband. Then one of the girls from the Abdullah clan brought a mirror and slowly reached around to hand it to the couple.

There in the mirror I watched these two people who would spend the rest of their lives together look at each other for the very first time. Tahir smiled broadly. Zeynab saw Tahir's reflection and for just a moment, she had the smallest look of surprise. Then she studied his face, his dark eyes, the firm line of his chin, and his warm smile. She smiled too – smiled beautifully because she was so beautiful.

For an instant she looked at me in the mirror,

and I, her sister, knew. Tahir was older even than she had expected. This was true. But she was happy. I nodded to the Abdullah girl and handed her my two corners of the shawl. Then I gave thanks to Allah for His book before I picked up the Holy Quran from the table. I held it above the heads of my sister and Tahir. Behind me, everyone went silent and in my heart I prayed for my sister's many future sons, for her husband to be kind, and for her happiness. After I passed the Holy Quran to Tahir, he kissed the book and opened it. He read a few of the sacred lines, placed money in the book, closed it, and then kissed it again. I accepted the book back from him and carefully placed it back on the table. With a nod to Khatira, I pulled back the shawl. My role in the arusi was finished.

Tahir and Zeynab held hands as they stood up and turned around to face everyone's cheers and applause. The band struck up another song and people moved about.

Khatira and I sat down next to Malehkah and Aunt Halima. I watched Zeynab and Tahir stare straight ahead with unsmiling faces for picture after picture, as was expected by custom. They cut into a huge cake before they fed each other crumbling pieces. I wanted to go speak to my sister, but Malehkah held me back.

"Stay out of the way and just watch."

When the music changed to something more spirited, many women took to dancing. I wanted to join them, but didn't like the thought of all those people staring at my mouth. I kept to myself with my chador covering me.

Malehkah rose to go get cake. "Here," she said when she returned. She handed me a plate with a piece of cake and the sweet bread powder called maleeda. "The cake is a bit too dry, but you should try to enjoy yourself."

"Bale, Madar," I whispered. She was right—the cake was the worst I'd ever had. I nodded to my father's wife. "Tashakor," I said, happy to have something to do besides sit and watch.

Later, Tahir went inside to the men's celebration, and my sister sat alone on the cushioned wooden couch, not allowed to join in the festivities at her own wedding. She nodded her thanks to each guest who congratulated her in turn. I waited for my chance to talk to her, but it never came. The line was too long. She sat right in front of me, and I already missed her.

Eventually, Gulzoma emerged through the glass double doors from the room where Zeynab had prepared for the arusi. Several women and girls, all of whom carried large platters piled with gifts, followed her. When she reached Zeynab's side, she clapped her hands and nodded for the band to quiet down. "Everyone, thank you for joining us for this wonderful occasion." She slid her arm around Zeynab's shoulders. "Tahir is simply overjoyed to have such a pretty young woman for his wife. It is time to see just how much he loves her by presenting the dowry!"

She held up a dark blue dress, then draped it over her arm. "Look at this dress! Such a beautiful deep blue! It almost matches mine. What's next?" She looked at another platter and smiled. "Ooooh, what a necklace! Let's just put this majestic gold on the lucky bride. In fact, there's so much jewelry, let's just put it all on this perfect doll right now!" She went on like that, showing off all the gifts, giving special attention to a chadri from Hajji Abdullah. There were at least three complete sets of new clothes and two chadris. My sister glittered with two gold bracelets and a pair of dangling gold earrings. Her sparkling gold necklace must have been heavy, thanks to the deep blue lapis lazuli pendant that hung from it.

When Gulzoma had finished revealing the gifts, Malehkah spoke quietly close to my ear. "It's tradition to offer a gift from the dowry to repay the hostess for her kindness." She groaned and stood up. When she reached Zeynab she bent down and reached around to the back of Zeynab's neck, whispering something in my sister's ear. Then she removed the lapis lazuli necklace and offered it to Gulzoma.

"What?" With a look of open-mouthed surprise on her face, Gulzoma held her hand to her chest.

"Tashakor, Gulzoma-jan, for such a beautiful wedding," Malehkah said.

"I just couldn't accept such a lovely necklace. I mean, I already have so many..." She put a finger to her lips. Then she shook her head and reached out to take the offering. "Zeynab is just so generous. How can I refuse such a kind gift?" She held the necklace up and people clapped. Then she nodded to the band and the music started up again.

"So much attention on gifts," I whispered when Malehkah returned.

My father's wife looked at me and spoke quietly. "Now you are beginning to understand."

After the sun had gone down and the stars sparkled brightly, Tahir returned and whispered something to Zeynab. They stood up together, her small delicate hand wrapped in his big, strong fingers. At once, all the women began clapping and whooping.

"Time to go," said Malehkah. I stood up with her and helped her into her chadri. We followed the couple to the front of the house, where we met Baba, my brothers, and the other men. My family walked close together, all of us except Zeynab, who would never walk with us again. If I could feel her absence this much here among this great crowd, how empty would life be at home without her? I shook my head and tried not to think of it. It was wrong to feel sad on such a happy occasion.

At the car, Malehkah's family said their goodbyes and offered to drive Uncle Ramin and his family to our house for the night. Then they'd drive home to Shindand. As for us, we would go to Tahir's house in Farah to say goodbye to Zeynab and to wish her well in her new home. Tahir and my sister climbed into his long white Toyota, which had been decorated in green, orange, and white ribbons and flowers.

In our Toyota, nobody spoke until my father started the engine. "HA! A wonderful day! Tahir Abdullah is a good man." Baba clapped his hands before shifting and swerving to get a good position close to the marriage car. "He's rich and getting richer! He will take good care of Zeynab, and he'll make a wonderful husband!"

I smiled at Baba's enthusiasm. Malehkah sat stiffly in the back seat with me, probably frowning under her chadri like she always did. Habib squirmed in my lap, trying to find a more comfortable position to sleep.

"And you, Zulaikha. Tahir tells me you did a marvelous job at the wedding. Tashakor. It's all so good! Tahir is lucky to have a nice, young wife instead of just those two old crones." My father laughed. Even quiet Najib smiled and chuckled a bit. Baba loosened his tie. "And thanks to some of the arrangements I've made with the Abdullahs, we're going to be making a lot of money!"

Malehkah turned to look at me. She patted Khalid, who was sitting between us, resisting sleep. She seemed to watch me for a long time through the mesh window in her chadri before she turned away and stared out the window. Our car rolled on through the dark desert, following the red tail lights of the car in which my sister rode with her new husband.

"See?" My father's shout jolted me awake. He ducked down so he could see Tahir's house past Najib on the passenger side. "What a fine big house. What did I tell you? Cement block walls. A second story being built even now. A fine match we've made for Zeynab."

We left the boys sleeping in the car and followed Tahir, Zeynab and Tahir's family... Zeynab's new family... up to the compound. Baba stopped and admired the house for just a moment, smiling and nodding before he led us inside. Feeling half asleep, I pulled my chador over my mouth as I entered the compound. Then the band started playing. Tahir had hired a band! A man smiled while he played a rubab. Another slapped out the rhythm on the tabla drums. A third squeezed and worked the keys of a sparkling harmonium as he sang about the greatness of Allah and the wonder of marriage. The cement pathway led across the courtyard to the cement front porch. Both the path and porch were lit by rows of candles on each side. After the women had removed their chadris, Tahir took my sister by the hand and walked her toward the house.

An older woman emerged from the front door. Her silver dress complemented her long gray hair. She grinned as a younger woman with shorter hair and a bluish green dress joined her. The first kept her smile as my sister climbed the two steps to the porch. "I'm Leena," said the older woman. "Welcome to our home."

"My name is Belquis." The second woman stepped

aside from the door. "Please come inside. We have tea ready. And food if you're hungry."

Tahir's wives showed us in, where a beautiful woven rug covered the floor and a platter stacked high with some naan, oranges, bananas, and pomegranates sat next to a teapot and about a dozen cups on a polished wooden table. A small electric light hung from the ceiling, and back in the shadows the family watched us. There were at least six small boys and girls. I also saw a girl my age and a couple of boys who looked a little younger. A young woman, maybe one of Leena's daughters, held a small baby of her own. I made sure to keep my mouth out of sight behind my chador.

Introductions were exchanged and most of the adults drank tea. Baba had an orange, but when none of the other adults ate, the children quickly took care of the food. I might have enjoyed some naan, but I didn't want to embarrass Zeynab in her new home by making everyone watch me eat. The music floated in from the courtyard outside and the conversation slowed.

Finally, Tahir slipped his hand around Zeynab's back. "Let me show you where you'll be sleeping." He led the way to what must have been his bedroom, and we all followed. "These are new blankets," said Tahir. He patted his incredibly big bed. It would be the first time my sister had ever slept on anything but a toshak.

I held the end of my chador up higher to cover my hot cheeks and tried not to think about my sister and Tahir. This was the way it was supposed to be, but it felt different seeing Tahir's bed. I turned and looked at Zeynab, trying to focus on something else.

Belquis stepped forward. She held out a hammer and nail to Zeynab, who was still smiling but shaking – nearly trembling. Malehkah had prepared her for this tradition before the shahba-henna. Standing up on her toes, she was just able to hold the nail to the top of the wooden door frame. With a number of timid taps at first, and then some harder hits, she drove her nail in beside two others. Zeynab's destiny was now fixed to this house, and to the man who owned it.

Baba smiled and shook Tahir's hand, pulling him closer and clapping him on the back with his other hand. "I'm very happy," said Baba. "These are good times."

Tahir nodded. "Bale, the very best."

"Khuda hafiz, Najib," said Zeynab. She hugged him. "I'll see you soon."

"Khuda hafiz," Najib said.

Baba hugged her next. "My beautiful daughter. I'm so happy for you. Everything has turned out perfect!"

Zeynab blushed and spoke quietly. "Tashakor, Baba-jan."

I wanted to make sure I was the last to say goodbye to my sister. I waited for Malehkah to say something, but she only pinched my elbow to remind me of what I must do.

I walked up to my sister in that dimly lit bedroom and quietly slipped her the wedding cloth. Before it became too awkward, I threw my arms around her. "I love you so much!" I blinked my eyes to try to hold back the tears. "I'm so happy for you." Even with my disfigured lips, I kissed Zeynab's cheek.

"I love you, too," Zeynab said. When I stepped back, she smiled. "Tashakor."

We went back to Baba's Toyota and then to An Daral, leaving my sister in her new home.

✦ ✦ ✦

Late the next morning, Jamila arrived at our compound carrying a cloth sack. She smiled at Malehkah and me and then pulled from the bag Zeynab's wedding cloth, stained with my sister's blood. Malehkah smiled, accepted the cloth, and thanked Jamila. Once she left, Malehkah's smile vanished.

"There," she said. "It is finished. Your sister is married." She handed me the cloth. "Now go burn this thing."

15

All my life, whenever I needed to talk about anything, I would go to Zeynab. When I had a question, I would ask her. When I was scared or worried, she would comfort me. When I needed someone to laugh or celebrate with, she was right with me. She was a line of protection against Malehkah and she was my best friend. My sister. We shared the same life, never separated.

Did she miss me like I missed her?

I couldn't ask her. I had seen her only three times since the wedding two weeks earlier – once at a party where we brought gifts to her in her new home, then at another party at Hajji Abdullah's, then at one more party in our house. All of these gatherings were supposed to unite our two families into one. I guess they did this, and I was excited to see my sister again, but with everyone else around, I didn't get the chance to talk to her. Not really. Not the way we used to talk.

When Zeynab and her new family had come to An Daral, I found one moment to talk to her alone in the kitchen. "Well, what's married life like? Is Tahir nice? What is it like to live with his other wives? I've missed you—"

"It's wonderful!" Zeynab's smile and the sound of her voice reminded me of the way she had tried to sweet-talk Khalid when we were watering the garden. She watched the door. "Everything I've ever hoped for and more!"

"Zeynab?" Tahir called from the main room.

My sister quickly snatched up the teapot she'd come to get and rushed out of the kitchen. That was my only chance to talk to her, and she hadn't even looked at me.

No matter how much I told myself that being married and having a family was what she had always dreamed about, no matter how much I tried to force the sad thoughts from my mind, I could not get past my loneliness.

Baba and Najib had their work and could talk to each other. Khalid and Habib played together. Malehkah never liked to say much to anyone. My unhappiness wasn't just doing the extra work that Zeynab used to do. I would have happily done twice as much work if it meant I could have someone to be with. Someone who understood me.

Now, after having taken Baba and Najib's midday meal to the construction site, I approached Meena's sewing shop. After what I had said to the muallem during my last visit, I doubted if she would even say more than a few words to me. But that was just it. I needed to hear something besides Malehkah's grumpy orders, my father's constant stream of business, and the whining of my little brothers.

I neared the shop door, reached out, and then dropped my hand and walked past. I couldn't go in there. Why should Meena talk to me after I'd been so mean to her?

"Change your mind, child?" Her voice came from behind me.

I stopped and faced her. She was standing on the packed-dirt walkway just outside her door. "What?"

"Did you change your mind about reading?"

"I don't know." I hesitated. At first I loved the poems, and I wanted to keep my promise to my mother. Then it all seemed like a waste... Now... "I really don't know."

"Ah, last time you were so certain," said Meena kindly. "Now it seems you need a cup of tea more than ever."

I followed her through her shop, past the faded curtain to the small space where she lived. She said nothing, but motioned for me to take my old seat in the green plastic chair. The faded black-and-white photograph of Meena's husband remained on the little table near her bed. The crack in the glass over the picture made it hard to see.

"How did you meet your husband?" I asked.

"What do you mean, child? I met Masoud at our wedding." She looked at me while she waited for the kettle to boil. "My second cousin's mother came to our house one day seeking a wife for her son. My parents thought it would be a suitable match."

"Were you happy?"

Meena smiled. "At first, I was nervous. Married for life to a man I'd never met! But my parents chose wisely. My years with Masoud were the happiest of my life. We loved each other. Had fun together. He even helped me through my studies so that I could become a professor at the university in Herat." The kettle began to whistle. She turned down the heat and poured the steaming hot water into the teapot. Then she took a book from a shelf and sat down on her bed, leafing through the pages. "Is that what this visit is about? Are you worried about your sister?"

I stared at the tiny wisp of steam rising from the spout of the teapot. The only sound was Meena flipping the old pages, one after another. "I don't know," I said. "She... I mean, all she ever dreamed about was being a good wife for a good man. Having a family." I shrugged. "She is happy. I should be happy for her."

"Are you?"

"I miss her."

Meena set the book aside, open to whatever point she had turned to. She stood up, poured two cups of tea, and handed one to me. I took it and dipped my head back to drink. She sat down and picked up her book. "Why are you here?"

I looked at her nearly white hair. Her aged face. Her deep, clear, sharp eyes. "I don't know," I said.

She nodded and lifted the book up to read.

"Oh, if Zulaikha only knew
A single wall kept her love from view!
A secret longing, a restless desire,
Burned through her blood and set her afire.
She tried to contain it, but she couldn't name
The light that had sparked this consuming flame."

"More from *Yusuf and Zulaikha*?" I asked. She nodded. "I feel like the poet is writing about me." Meena smiled. I shook my head. "I'm not just talking about him using my name. I mean, this part is about Zulaikha missing someone. And it's about…"

"Missing something else?"

"Yes. A secret longing. A restless desire." I searched for the right words, grateful that Meena was patient enough to wait for them. "Zeynab is married. That's a wonderful thing." I touched my split lip. "I was supposed to have this fixed. Only I didn't get my surgery, and somehow my sister's marriage hasn't made me happy." I took a drink, hoping that Muallem would say just the right thing. Instead, she still waited for me to speak. "I'm sorry," I said. "I've been thinking about what I said the last time I was here. I didn't mean it." I wanted to explain everything. "I'm sorry" was all I could say.

Muallem held up her hand. "No apologies, child. You are learning."

I took a drink. "I think I want to keep learning." I wanted it if only for the pleasure of having someone to talk to, that much I understood. "I want to be able to read and write on my own. The poems were important to my mother. To you too." I looked up at Muallem.

"I want to learn more about them."

"What's more," Meena smiled, "the words, the old poems, are a great comfort to us when we are lonely. Now, let us look at this bit of *Yusuf and Zulaikha* that I just read from. We'll explore the sounds the letters make and examine in particular some of the simpler words." She looked up from the page. "Ready?"

"Bale, Muallem-sahib."

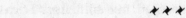

"This lamb," my father said later that night, sucking the juice from his fingers as we all sat around the dastarkhan to eat, "is really good, Zulaikha."

"Tashakor," I said, trying to remember the last time he'd complimented Malehkah's cooking. Or Zeynab's. I looked at the empty space next to me.

"You keep cooking like this, and you'll make your husband really happy some day." He picked up a bone and gnawed on the little bit of meat left on it. "Mmm. So good." Malehkah stared at Baba for a moment. When Habib reached for more naan, she tore off a strip for him. Baba dropped the bone in front of him. "Kind of quiet without Zeynab around. If she's cooking half this good, then Tahir must be a very happy man! Ah, speaking of Tahir..." – Baba pointed at Najib – "I still need you to take the Toyota to the bazaar tonight and pick up the steel I ordered. Tahir wants that second block press machine finished by the end of the week."

"Bale, Baba," said Najib.

With a sigh, I rolled rice into a little ball in my fingers. I was about to lean my head back to eat, but my father was watching me with a frown. He seemed to miss Zeynab too, at least a little bit. Maybe he'd take me to see her.

I took a deep breath. "Baba-jan, do you think—"

"You know," Baba said. "Hajji Abdullah hasn't had a moment's peace since the wedding." He rubbed his knuckles against his chin. "It seems that his first wife always pesters him and asks if it is still possible to get you to the Americans in Kandahar for your surgery." He grinned. "He talked to that woman soldier in Farah. She says they're expecting a flight tomorrow. I figure Najibullah can take you there. We can spare him for three or four days. Maybe we'll get you all fixed up after all."

I dropped the rice I'd been holding and stared at my father, wide-eyed. Then I looked at Najib, who seemed as surprised as I was. Baba-jan sounded like a cannon when he burst into laughter. "What? Not even a 'tashakor'?"

"Really, Baba-jan?" I asked. "Tomorrow?"

Baba laughed until his face was red. I scrambled to my feet, sidestepping a clapping Khalid to run to my father's outstretched arms. Baba squeezed me close. "That's my good, sweet girl, Zulaikha. Everything will be perfect very soon."

I buried my face in my father's chest, almost afraid that if I let him go, the chance for the surgery and a normal mouth would be snatched away again.

Later that night, after the dishes and the evening prayer were done, I tried to sleep on my toshak up on the roof. Reaching out to the empty space next to me, I wished I could hold Zeynab's hand. My chest ached with the need to share this wonderful news with her.

A spark of light, a shooting star, fell across the starscape, a bright trail burning behind it. Had Zeynab seen it too? I had been praying for her happiness in her marriage. Maybe she had prayed for my surgery. How else could this miracle be explained?

But I worried, because I had thought all of these happy thoughts before and then my hopes were wasted on a helicopter that never came. I prayed and prayed that this time would be different. I didn't know how I could deal with the disappointment again if it wasn't.

I must have slept, because Najib shook me awake and said simply, "Zulaikha." It was still very dark. I looked to the mountains in the east and could not see even the faintest hint of dawn. We were awake impossibly early, well before the call of the muezzin. I snapped to action, jumping up off my toshak and hurrying after my brother down the steps into our house. I expected all to be dark. Instead, everyone was gathered in the center room, which was brightened by our kerosene lamp. In my sleepiness and hurry, I hadn't even noticed that Khalid and Habib weren't up on the roof.

"Good luck, Zulaikha," Khalid said.

Habib said nothing, but kept his small stubby arms wrapped tightly around my legs until Khalid pulled him away. My smallest brother wiped his sleepy eyes and then waved at me.

"Be good for the Americans, Zulaikha. Make sure you thank them. Do what they say," said Malehkah. When our eyes met, my father's wife only nodded deeply before we both looked away.

Last of all, Baba-jan picked me up in a tremendous, warm hug. He lifted me off the floor and held me as he hadn't held me in years. He kissed my cheek and then set me down.

"Don't you worry, Zulaikha. Najibullah will make sure you are safe on your journey. Then when your mouth is all better and you come back to us, I promise you we will all celebrate! Didn't I say before that these are good times?" Baba-jan rubbed my back and then tossed his keys to Najib. My brother nodded to me and we went outside, and then we were finally in the car and on our way.

After we passed through An Daral, Najib gripped the steering wheel tightly. "I'm trying to remember the way to Farah. It all looks different in the dark." He didn't say anything else the entire trip. Eventually, we did reach the city, where we drove through the dark, empty, early morning streets and out to the American base. When our headlights struck the wire, the whole base looked even more frightening and unwelcoming than it did the first time I was there.

When we parked by the checkpoint, Najib's hands shook as he fingered his prayer beads, sliding each bead one at a time along the loop of string. An Afghan guard approached our car, took one look at me, and announced us over his radio. Then he asked us to turn off the engine and wait. Finally, I could see the headlights of a vehicle approaching. A little pickup stopped next to our car, and Captain Mindy and Shiaraqa stepped out.

"*Salaam*, Zulaikha," said Captain Mindy. Najib looked at me. I shrugged and we stepped out of our car. "*Salaaaaaaam*!" she repeated and reached out to my brother. Najib hesitated for a moment and then finally shook the woman's hand. "*What name*?" Captain Mindy was still trying to speak in her crazy-sounding Dari. Najib looked at me again.

"This is Captain Mindy," I said quietly. "I think she wants to know your name."

My brother looked at the ground when he spoke. "Najibullah."

The captain smiled. "Najibullah?" Then she said something in English.

Shiaraqa spoke. "She says she is happy you understood her when she asked for your name." Najibullah shrugged. Shiaraqa translated again. "She welcomes you to Farah Base."

Captain Mindy smiled, crouched in front of me, and then reached to shake my hand. I did as she expected. At least she'd paid attention to my brother first. Maybe she was learning. "*Tashakor*!" She sounded like she was talking to a baby.

Shiaraqa translated for the captain. "She says all the soldiers here on the base have been looking forward to this day." He smiled, but looked like he was having trouble keeping up with everything the excited American was saying. He turned to my brother. "Your car will be safe here at the outer checkpoint. We'll ride in our truck. You two can sit in the back. The captain and I will ride up front."

"Bale" was all Najib said. He sounded like I usually did after Malehkah shouted at me.

We rode right up through the gate. This time there were no soldiers to search us the way they'd searched Baba-jan on our first visit. Shiaraqa explained that it was too early in the morning for soldiers to be on gate duty. He added that Captain Mindy was supposed to search us, but she trusted us and hated searching anyway. We stopped only so that Shiaraqa could get out and bolt the gate shut behind us.

Inside the base, we were led into a tan, one-story building. The captain spoke. "She says this is the nicest building on the base," Shiaraqa translated.

It took a moment for my eyes to adjust to the bright light, but I was surprised to find myself in a space far different than the small medical room I'd seen before. This place looked much more Afghan, with pretty rugs on the floors and a red, green, and black Afghan flag on the wall, next to a framed photograph of President Hamid Karzai.

Captain Mindy motioned for us to have a seat on one of several padded wooden couches that surrounded a low wooden table. She pointed to a tray of different types of nuts, looking sad as she said something. I held my chador tight to my mouth, hoping she didn't have bad news. Shiaraqa explained. "She asks Najibullah to please enjoy some nuts, but she says that Zulaikha must not eat before the surgery. It is what the doctor commands."

I put my hands over my stomach, feeling it rumble. How long would it be until the surgery? I sat down close to my brother, keeping my chador across my face. The captain leaned toward me and spoke in a high-pitched voice with a smile that wrinkled her freckled nose. Shiaraqa looked at her once before speaking. "She asks if you are excited."

I shifted in my seat. I said softly, "Bale."

Captain Mindy smiled again and told us through Shiaraqa that the weather was good and so far the flight was still coming. Apparently, nobody at Farah

223

knew when the helicopter was supposed to arrive. Sometimes they were early. Sometimes they were late. She only hoped the flight wouldn't be canceled.

As soon as Shiaraqa translated the words, my nerves mixed with my hunger and I worried I would be sick. This was the second time Baba and Hajji Abdullah had been troubled with my surgery. If the flight were canceled now, there would be no other chances. I prayed over and over, the same prayer:

Great Allah, the most merciful, please let the helicopter come. Please let the helicopter come.

We waited. They brought a hot meal for my brother, who only ate some of the potatoes. I stared at the food. I was grateful for my chador when my mouth watered.

We waited. More and more soldiers came and went, all of them very happy, many of them bringing me toys and candy of all kinds. More small metal cars. Some fuzzy animal toys. A plastic doll with blonde hair and very long legs. I didn't know how to react. I'd never been given so many presents in my life, so I simply thanked them as Captain Mindy put their gifts into a plastic bag for me. All the while, Najib said nothing, but kept looking down. He spoke only when he was asked a direct question. Sitting so close to him,

I could feel his legs shaking. Our past had made us both very nervous about people with guns.

As sunlight began to shine in through the windows from outside, I realized that I'd missed the morning prayer. I hadn't even heard the muezzin. The Americans really were infidels if they couldn't even hear the call to prayer from their base. I went back to my silent prayers, rocking just a little as I asked Allah for His forgiveness and His help.

Finally, after Captain Mindy had repeatedly sent soldiers to check to see if the flight would still happen, her radio squawked with someone speaking in English. Shiaraqa suddenly stood up and stretched. The captain smiled. I did not need to wait for Shiaraqa's translation. The helicopter was coming.

Once again we rode in a truck across the base, but this time we were taken to a different metal gate on the opposite side of the compound. When we got out of the truck, I couldn't see the helicopter yet, but I could hear it in the distance, perhaps on the other side of the closest mountain. It was a faint but growing *whoo, whoo, whoo* sound. Six or seven American soldiers were gathered near us with their guns and some big green bags.

Then at last we could see the helicopter, the size of

a large truck, with two whirling blades, one on each end. As it approached, the roar from its spinning rotors grew. It hovered a moment, then lowered itself down onto a cement platform well outside the compound gate. A great wave of dust blew toward us. Everyone closed their eyes, bent their heads, and did their best to shield themselves from the flying grit.

Almost as soon as the helicopter landed, Captain Mindy grabbed my arm and pulled me forward while Shiaraqa led my brother. If I had lost my nerve and changed my mind about taking a ride in this big machine, it wouldn't have mattered. I was pulled quickly through the chaos under the spinning blades and then lifted up a big step onto a ramp that led through the back hatch to the floor of the aircraft. Soldiers ran in and out, loading and unloading bags and boxes.

On the outside, the helicopter was graceful and futuristic. Inside, there were exposed cables and metal tubes. I didn't have long to look around, though. Everyone sat down on cloth seats with their backs against the wall, four to each side. The captain reached over and clicked a strap into place over my lap.

Then I felt like I was being pushed down into my seat as the aircraft rose. It was like nothing I'd ever known before. I had to lean forward to see around Najib, who himself leaned forward to see around the Americans. Out the back hatch, the view of the ground transformed. The four white walls that formed the gigantic square of the American compound shrank until the big trucks inside it looked even smaller than my brothers' toy metal cars. The aircraft tilted, and I felt like I was swinging on a rope.

The highest I'd ever been before was atop the walls at the Citadel, and then I was, for the most part, solidly connected to the earth. Now I was soaring far above the ground in this enormous machine. How did anyone make something so large and heavy fly through the sky? Below, tiny farms and villages were islands in a sea of fields and dust, until gradually there were no more fields. There was only dust, and then the red-brown crags of mountains.

Shiaraqa shouted something to Captain Mindy over the engine noise. When she nodded, he got up out of his seat and moved about the aircraft. Najib watched him eagerly until Shiaraqa came and unbuckled my brother's seat strap. Then both of them walked around, cautiously in the beginning, and then more relaxed, delightedly pointing out interesting sights through the open back hatch. I was scared for them at first.

The soldier sitting on the deck behind the machine gun, with his legs dangling out the hatch, was tethered in with a long strap. Nothing was holding Shiaraqa and Najib. But Shiaraqa took picture after picture with a small camera in his hand, so it must have been safe enough.

Captain Mindy laughed at their excitement. She and I exchanged a look, and then we both laughed at the two dewana Afghan men.

After that, Captain Mindy laid her head back and rode peacefully with her eyes closed. Most of the soldiers slept, but Najib and I stayed awake the entire time, watching our country from the sky all the way. The deep, dark reds of the high rocky mountaintops and the lighter browns of the valleys and dry plains looked like Allah's beautiful painting from up here. It was Afghanistan, my home.

When we had flown for a long time, we could see roads and buildings again, and I could feel the helicopter begin to descend. My stomach felt tight and there was a light burning in my throat. My brother nodded his head toward the view out the hatch and I knew – I knew we were approaching Kandahar. We were close to the time for my surgery.

16

After our helicopter landed, Najib and I followed
Captain Mindy and Shiaraqa out of the machine. I put
my hand up to shield my eyes from the glare of the
sun. In front of us, waves of heat rose off an enormous
paved road as wide as two or three rows of compounds
and at least twice as long as An Daral's bazaar road.
Half a kilometer away sat a row of helicopters just like
the one we had flown in on. I counted at least ten. In
a row behind those were different helicopters, smaller
ones with only one big propeller on top. But on the
bottoms of these were big guns and tube things that
might have been bombs.

I felt a hand on my shoulder and spun around.
Najib tilted his head toward Captain Mindy and
Shiaraqa, who waited a few paces away. Stupid!
Shiaraqa had told us to follow him, and here I was
counting helicopters. It was just that yesterday I'd
never even seen a helicopter, except for once or twice
on a television in the bazaar. Today I had ridden

on one and seen dozens more. I pulled my chador over my face.

Najib took my hand and we followed Captain Mindy and Shiaraqa down a different, much narrower paved street. Only cars, trucks, and American gun trucks drove on this road. Wooden buildings, tents, and parked vehicles lined either side of the street.

As we walked, I was confused to see soldier after soldier snapping their right hand up to the edge of their hats with their palms down. As they did this they would say something in English, and then Captain Mindy would make the same gesture. Finally, after more than thirty soldiers had done this, Captain Mindy began the exchange with an older-looking man she was about to pass.

Shiaraqa dropped back from the captain's side and quietly explained to my brother, "They do this thing with their hand to show respect to whoever has more rank, to whoever is more important. They say good afternoon, or good evening, or whatever time of day it is when they salute in this way."

Najib's voice was hardly above a whisper. "Should we do this too?"

Shiaraqa laughed. "No. It is just something the Americans do. Captain Edmanton says most soldiers don't even like to do it." He shrugged. "But that is the rule for the base."

We rounded a corner, crossed the street, and passed the end of a row of dusty tents, and that is when I saw it. "Najib," I whispered, and tugged at my brother's sleeve. But of course he saw it too. It was too large to miss. And too beautiful.

A mosque. But not just any mosque. It was easily twice as large as the mud-brick mosque back in An Daral. Red, blue, green, and black tiles shone on the tall columns in front. The windows had glass and were framed in pretty blue. The towering minaret had little blue-trimmed window holes with a blue dome on top, and I could see huge speakers inside. Nobody could fail to hear the call to prayer from this mosque.

It gleamed in the sun as an omen from Allah. The day I had prayed for my whole life was here. Inshallah, all would be well.

Finally, we reached a large two-story cement building. Bumps rose on my skin and a shiver crawled up my back into my neck the moment I stepped inside and out of the bright sun. We'd been led into a room with a smooth cement floor, white walls, and long tubes of electric lights suspended from the high ceiling. I pulled my chador tighter around me and looked at Najib. He folded his arms around himself and shrugged. Captain Mindy motioned for us to stay where we were while she went down the hall.

"They have air-conditioning." Shiaraqa took off his black sunglasses. "The Americans don't like it so hot. And they have to keep their computers cool." He shook the dust from his thick black hair, wiping his hands on his jeans afterwards.

Soon the captain returned and led us around a corner to where soldiers were busy working at their desks. "In here," Shiaraqa said. We entered a small room with white walls and a big desk covered in papers. A soldier was at the desk, pressing buttons on what must have been his computer. I sat down next to Najib in one of the two plastic chairs. Captain Mindy and Shiaraqa sat next to the other wall. The man looked up from his work.

Shiaraqa translated for Captain Mindy. "Zulaikha, Najibullah, this is Doctor Akamura. He will be the one conducting your surgery."

"*Salaam*," said the doctor. He was a compact man dressed in a tan uniform just like the rest of the soldiers, but he was older than most Americans I had seen. His close-cropped black hair was flecked with gray, especially at the sides of his head.

When he smiled he almost closed his eyes.

Shiaraqa translated Doctor Akamura's words. "He says he is very happy to meet you both, Najibullah, Zulaikha." He addressed my brother first, which was at least somewhat closer to Afghan custom than I was used to with Americans. "He will be the one taking care of Zulaikha's cleft lip. He wants to tell you both a little about the procedure, and then both of you can ask any questions you wish."

The doctor went on talking about what he planned to do, pausing every now and then to allow Shiaraqa to catch up and translate. The doctor seemed nice, but why was he bothering to explain all of this? He was, after all, the doctor. He was the one who was going to be doing the work. What difference did it make if I knew how he was going to do it?

Finally, Shiaraqa asked if we had any questions. Najib was back to staring at the floor. After a moment of quiet, Shiaraqa translated for the doctor again. "This operation will not hurt very much. Soon you will have a good smile and you will not need to cover your face."

Captain Mindy spoke, the doctor answered, and Shiaraqa translated for them both. "She asks him how long it will take you to recover and when you can go home. He says you can go home in one or two days."

At this news, I glanced at my brother. He looked up just enough so that his wide eyes met mine. They had told us before that this wouldn't be a long trip, but it still didn't seem real. How could they fix my mouth and have me back home in so short a time?

I clenched my fist in my lap and remembered the sun glinting off the mosque outside. I had to have patience. Patience and faith.

"He says that you can wait in the room down the hall. They will be ready to start in an hour or two," Shiaraqa said.

We were led to a small room where Shiaraqa started a movie on a television. He explained that all the characters were cartoons made on a computer. Then he translated the first part of the show for us until he and Captain Mindy went to eat. Najib was invited along, but he shook his head and stayed with me. I was very hungry, but of course I wasn't allowed to eat or do anything that might interfere with the operation. Instead, I watched this program about how a rich American boy's toys come to life when nobody is looking and have adventures all around his giant house.

"Khalid and Habib would like to watch these toy army men." It was only the second thing Najib had said to me since we left Farah.

I laughed. "Bale, Najib. But Habib might be afraid of the little, fat brown rock man. The way his stick-on eyes and ears keep falling off."

My brother shrugged. "Rock man? I thought he was supposed to be donkey poop."

We both laughed at this. I couldn't remember a time I had seen Najib laugh that hard. It was good to see him so happy.

The laughter helped me relax. I didn't know if the surgery would work, but the Americans were going to give it a try. This was my chance to be normal, to maybe one day be a happy bride, smiling at the reflection of my husband in the mirror, the way my beautiful sister had smiled at her wedding. It was really going to happen.

Finally, Captain Mindy returned with Shiaraqa. "She says the doctor is ready."

I followed them down the hall. My brother gently touched my shoulder. I turned to him and he bent down to whisper to me. "I will pray for you, Zulaikha. You are a good sister." He squeezed my shoulder.

Captain Mindy took my right hand in hers.

She smiled down at me. "Don't be afraid." Shiaraqa translated her soft words, some of the warmth in her English also coming through in his Dari. "You won't feel a thing, and we'll all be right here with you when you wake up."

I walked into a cold room with bright lights over a table in its center. Doctor Akamura wore a green uniform with a little mask hanging from his neck.

I was asked to go behind a curtain to change into a funny dress that tied in the back. I was very careful to keep my backside hidden away from everyone. Captain Mindy must have understood what I was nervous about, because she helped to hold the dress closed while I slid up on the table. I was cold, and I felt scared and naked in that tiny dress. This was true. But if I had to wear that stupid thing for the Americans to fix me, it was something I'd have to live with.

I looked for Najib and found him standing next to Shiaraqa at the edge of the room. An American woman who was wearing the same blue-green outfit as the doctor gently pushed me back on the table. Shiaraqa told me that the doctor wanted me to lie down, breathe deeply, and relax. Were they crazy? How could I relax at this moment?

The rest happened quickly. A little cold wet cloth

was rubbed in a circle on my arm. Shiaraqa warned me I would feel a little pinch, and then I sucked in a breath as a needle was pushed into my arm. Captain Mindy spoke in English. I couldn't understand her words, but the soft sounds she made helped me calm down. She slowly breathed in and out, and I did the same.

A plastic mask was placed over my face. Shiaraqa said again that Doctor Akamura wanted me to breathe deep, relax, and go to sleep. So I breathed deep. I tried to relax. But as excited as I was, I knew I would never sleep.

17

The room had changed. The bright light above the table was gone. I wasn't so cold any more. The young American woman who was standing next to me just a moment ago had left. I ran my tongue around my dry mouth and cringed at the metal taste, feeling a dull ache in my teeth and lips. Were they done with the surgery? Impossible. I had only just climbed up on the table. But the needle… It was no longer in my arm. And my mouth…

I slowly reached my hand up to my face, gently touching my top lip. My lip. I touched my lip. Not an ugly split. Not twisted teeth. My lip.

"Najib?"

It hurt a little to speak, but in a moment he leaned over above me. He smiled big. "Salaam." Najib gently pushed my hand away from my face. "How do you feel?"

"Sleepy." I tried to sit up but my head whirled and I lay back down. "Dizzy." My words sounded strange – not that I could ever speak right. Yet they sounded a different sort of funny than usual.

In the next instant, my brother was gone and Captain Mindy was looking down at me. She made some friendly, soothing sounds in English. Then she vanished.

Finally, dimly aware that time had passed, I sat up so that I was resting on my elbows. Najib saw me and jumped from his chair to rush to my side. "Are you awake for good now?"

"Was I asleep?"

He nodded. "You kept waking up and then going back to sleep."

I squinted my eyes shut and then opened them to focus. I had a thought that I might be dreaming. But everything felt very real, including the throbbing in my lip.

"The surgery worked." Najib smiled, turned, and reached for something on a nearby table. He handed me a mirror. "Go on, look. You won't believe it. Allahu Akbar! God is good!"

I took in a breath and held the mirror up. I could hardly look. My vision blurred with tears. "My mouth…"

"They say the swelling will go away and then you

will look just fine." Najib glanced around as if to see if anyone else was listening. He whispered, "They say you will look very pretty."

"Oh. My mouth." There was a vertical line of tiny stitches running from the middle of my puffy upper lip to my nose, but I had an upper lip. No more did my teeth stick out and show. "My mouth. Najib." For the first time in my life, I could almost make the *b* sound and say my brother's name properly. I could not hold back my tears.

My brother grinned and squeezed my shoulder. I looked at him and smiled back, though it hurt a little to do so. "No... more... Donkeyface." I pushed the words out through happy sobs. Najib could only nod. "Praise Allah. My mouth."

✶ ✶ ✶

The rest of the day was spent lying in a puffy bed high off the floor, watching American movies. We watched the toy movie again and then we watched a second toy movie. Eventually, I stopped paying attention. There were many visits from Doctor Akamura, Captain Mindy, and Shiaraqa. My brother never left my side, but stayed in a cushioned chair near my bed. I was surprised at how good I felt. It was such an amazing change for so little pain. The dull ache remained, and I hated the smell and feel of the slimy clear cream they made me keep on my mouth, but other than that, I felt fine by nightfall.

I'm not sure the Americans believed me when I told them that, though. Again and again they asked how I was feeling. And they brought me gifts, even the Americans I had never seen before. They filled another plastic sack full of candy (for when I was better), dolls (for me or my sister), and toy cars and planes (for my brothers). I thanked them again and again, but didn't they understand how useless these trinkets were compared to the priceless gift of my new mouth?

Finally, Doctor Akamura bowed to me with his hand over his heart. Shiaraqa translated as the doctor spoke. "The doctor believes the operation was a complete success. He says your recovery should be short. He must leave now to take a plane to Kabul, but he hopes you will have a very happy life."

Najib's grin was warmer than I'd ever seen. "*Thank you. Thank you.*" He tried his best to speak English. He gave the doctor a "thumbs-up" sign. "*Thank you.*"

The doctor shook my brother's hand. He nodded

to Captain Mindy on his way to the door. "*Khuda hafiz*," he said as he left. Captain Mindy had Shiaraqa tell us that she was going to walk the doctor to the plane.

I couldn't stop checking my face in the mirror. The more the swelling went down, the more normal I looked. I took a deep breath in through my nose, which the surgery had also straightened. If only Zeynab could be here! She'd be so happy. And I could smile, really smile, with her. I wondered, for a moment, if I looked more like my sister. Could I look even a little bit pretty? If I could have such a miracle surgery, surely anything was possible. Anything.

But by lunchtime the next day, at least part of my excitement was wearing off. I was hungry and tired of eating this red wiggly stuff they called Jell Oh. It was tasty enough, but I longed for real food – a warm piece of naan and some rice, maybe even an orange. After all, my mouth no longer throbbed with pain as it did the day before. Now it only hurt when I pushed on my lip. I bit my finger to test my teeth. I would probably have trouble with a tough piece of meat, but otherwise I felt ready to eat.

I was glad, then, when Captain Mindy and Shiaraqa finally came to tell me to put my own clothes back on. Shiaraqa smiled when he translated for the captain. "She says we will fly home soon, but first we must go eat at the place they call the chow hall. If you are feeling well enough, you can have as much food as you like. They have everything. It is almost like a whole bazaar of food, all for free!"

Najib raised his eyebrows at the interpreter.

After I dressed, we followed Captain Mindy and Shiaraqa across the base to a wooden building. Inside, Captain Mindy held up a piece of paper and led us to the front of a long line of soldiers. "Don't worry," she said through Shiaraqa. "You'll love it."

Captain Mindy gave us each our own plastic tray. We went through a long, clean room with a shiny tiled floor, and passed a glass case filled with different hot dishes. I didn't see any food I recognized and felt my stomach gurgle with hunger and nervousness.

Shiaraqa held his tray up for the woman behind the counter and asked for something. Then he turned to my brother and me and pointed at the various foods. "This is called a hamburger. It is made from cow meat and you eat it between two pieces of American bread called buns." He waved away the food in the next big pan. "Don't eat that. They are called tenderloins but they are really just pig meat. The peas are okay. Here are smashed potatoes. I'm having fried chicken too.

The Americans at Farah love this. It is very good."

I shrugged at my brother, held my tray up, and asked Shiaraqa if he would get just a little piece of chicken for me. Then Captain Mindy said something. "She says to remember there is more food through there." Shiaraqa nodded to an archway in the center wall of the big room. Najib pointed to the chicken and potatoes, hardly looking up as though he was afraid they would not give him any food.

The captain told us to follow her. We entered a large room full of Americans sitting at tables, talking and eating. In the corner up on the wall was a television four times the size of the one I had been watching in the hospital. The American President was on, much larger than a normal person on that big screen. Then the show switched to two men sitting at a desk talking. All the while at the bottom of the screen, words or maybe numbers whizzed by. Captain Mindy waved at us and then pointed to another food line as if to ask me if I wanted anything.

"That's ham. More pig meat," Shiaraqa said, making sure Captain Mindy put down one of my meat selections. The captain stepped aside and let Shiaraqa pick the food. "Here is some roast beef." He used a sort of plastic gripper to place the meat on a piece of bread. Then he used a different plastic gripper to put on some lettuce and still another for a slice of tomato. When he was finished, he put another piece of bread on top of the stack and smiled. "The Americans call this a *sandwich*."

"*Sandwich*," I whispered. Najib made a sandwich for himself. Then we all selected drinks from a refrigerator and sat down at a table near another glass case full of something Captain Mindy called *pie*.

It was time to test my mouth and teeth. Captain Mindy, Shiaraqa, and Najib all ate quickly for a few minutes, but I took my time, lifting the sandwich the way Captain Mindy held hers. I brought it up, opened my mouth, and bit down on one corner. My teeth were a little sore, so I had to eat slowly and carefully, but it was working! My front teeth cut through the food until I had a bite in my mouth and could chew. The sandwich was cold, but the flavors of all the foods in the stack mixed well. I placed my lips on the rim of the can of soda and tried drinking. I could hold the sweet soda in my mouth without tilting my head back. I could eat and drink like everyone else. Nobody was staring at me as they did when I used to have to eat like a bird. Nobody in the whole crowded hall even noticed me.

Captain Mindy eventually said something, though. "She says you are eating very well. That is very good," Shiaraqa said.

We ate the rest of the meal in that loud chow hall without speaking, and by the time I finished all my food, I was very full. The soda I drank was not quite as sweet as Zam Zam, but it was more bubbly, and made me feel as though I might burst.

Finally, the captain looked at her watch and said it was time to go. She led us through the double doors. Next to the walls on either side of us were two large buckets almost as big as me. These buckets were lined with open plastic bags, and Captain Mindy showed us how to scrape any food we had not eaten into the buckets before we put our trays on a small table. I had only one chicken bone to put in the can.

At that moment a soldier came out with his tray, picking his teeth. He nodded at Captain Mindy before he scraped his extra food into the bucket. I watched him dump out a whole sandwich and a banana. How could he do it? There were too many poor and hungry Afghans for us to throw away food. Wasting it was considered almost a crime. If somehow there was food left that spoiled so that it could not be eaten, we still saved it to feed to our cow, Torran. But there in the big black plastic bag were kilos and kilos of perfectly good food.

I looked at Najib, who must have been as disgusted as I was, because he shook his head. Captain Mindy and Shiaraqa, on the other hand, walked on by like nothing had happened. We followed them out of the building and across the base, to where we would wait for our helicopter.

✦ ✦ ✦

The flight home was much like our first flight, bored Americans sleeping and Shiaraqa and Najib moving around trying to get the best views. I sat in my seat feeling tired but excited as the moment for showing off my fixed lip to my family drew closer and closer.

After the helicopter touched down outside the south gate of the American base at Farah, Captain Mindy walked Najib and me to the front gate and out to Baba's car. Through Shiaraqa she repeated the instructions for keeping my mouth clean and for the cream I was supposed to put on my lip every day so I wouldn't get sick. She looked at me in a kind way that reminded me of Meena, or my mother, or Zeynab.

A few days ago, I was just an ugly girl from a small village with a mangled mouth. Now I'd flown around the skies in an American helicopter. I'd walked around their Kandahar base. My mouth was fixed. Even with the swelling, I looked almost normal. And I had the Americans, as ignorant and wasteful as they were, to thank.

"Tashakor," I said, wishing I could think of better words, in Dari or in English, to express how I felt.

Captain Mindy put her arms around me. This time, I hugged her back. She said some kind words to me in English. Shiaraqa did not translate. No translation was needed.

✦ ✦ ✦

As soon as I got out of the car, Baba-jan wrapped me in his big powerful arms and swept me up off the ground in a great hug. "Allahu Akbar! God is great! Look at what they've done for my baby girl! Look, Khalid. Look, everyone! Come see how they've changed Zulaikha!" His eyes glowed with the same fire of excitement as the day he announced his job on the school. He smelled of the sweat and dust and welding slag from a hard day working, and I could draw it all in through my repaired nose. I rested my head against his chest. I was too old to be held up like little Habib, but I loved being surrounded by my father's arms. Baba-jan, sweet, good Baba-jan, was making my transformation all I had ever dreamed about.

His thick, rough-skinned hand rested on my forehead and he gently pushed my head up off of his chest. "No, no, Zulaikha, no more hiding away. My beautiful daughter." He set me down and turned me to face the rest of the family.

Khalid stood on his toes, stretching his neck one way and another, trying to look closer. When I smiled at him with a real smile, he gasped and roughly pulled Habib closer so he could see. Habib was more interested in Baba's excitement. He clapped his hands and giggled until Khalid grabbed his head and forced him to look at me. Habib squinted, looking carefully. He pointed to his own mouth and then mine, smiling.

"Wah wah, 'Laikha!" said Habib.

The look on my youngest brother's face made my eyes ache with the pressure of holding back joyful tears.

Malehkah, sitting on the front porch with her

hands over her swollen belly, nodded to me. "You look better."

From Malehkah, this was high praise. If only Zeynab were here to see me transformed, everything would be perfect.

Baba-jan clapped his hands. "Tonight, we celebrate! Malehkah, we must have the biggest feast. We'll eat all the best of everything." He put his arm around Najib's shoulders. "Come, Najibullah, I have some plans for the Nimruz Clinic that I want to show you!" Baba-jan led Najib around the house to the back courtyard to talk about men's business.

Malehkah squinted her eyes and wrinkled her nose at me, and I noticed she was looking not at me, but at my mouth. This is how she'd always looked at me. But this time, there was a difference. Though she scowled, there was a hint of an upturn to her lips. Not a smile, but not really a frown either. She shook her head and went into the house.

I leaned back against the compound wall in the quiet front courtyard, letting the warm sunlight shine on my face. I was home. And for the first time in my life, I felt whole.

18

The next two months blurred into one long endless stream of work. Afghanistan held a big election for Parliament. Baba was pretty excited for it. He even insisted that Malehkah vote, saying it was important for everyone to exercise their new rights. But I think he also told Malehkah to vote for those candidates whose ideas might lead to more welding and construction contracts.

I couldn't make myself care about the election. Malehkah's coming baby made her tired quickly. That left me to take care of the entire household. I looked after the boys. I cleaned and dusted. I went to the bazaar. I cooked most of the meals. I fed and milked Torran. I cleaned her stall. I watered and weeded the garden in the morning and evening.

Most nights, I collapsed on my toshak tired and alone. In the morning, when I woke, I still missed my sister. I had asked Baba several times if he would take me to visit Zeynab, but he always said he was too busy and we'd go as soon as his work schedule slowed down. Sometimes I'd think about all the things I wanted to tell Zeynab, about how wonderful it was to be able to go to the bazaar without worrying about everyone staring at my mouth, about how the business contracts from her bride-price were bringing Baba so much success, keeping him busy and happy. Then I'd think of all the work that I would have to do that day. And the next day. And the day after that.

My only breaks were the short lessons I was able to sneak with Meena. Since I went to the bazaar often, I had been to her shop many times, showing the muallem what I had copied, sounding out words, and even putting whole sentences together.

Now I was fighting the one war Afghanistan could never win – the battle against dust. The Winds of 120 Days had died down, but even so, everything in the house somehow ended up covered in sandy grit. Because of this, I found myself dusting everything in the house over and over again.

I wiped the sweat from my upper lip as I dusted off trunks in the storage room. Inside my own trunk next to me was the notebook from Captain Mindy. I took it out and turned to the page of poetry that Meena had recited, then I took the pen that I had clipped to the notebook cover and began to copy the lines again. Right to left, the swoops and dots and swirls formed words across the page.

Oh, if Zulaikha only knew
A single wall kept her love from view!
A secret longing, a restless desire,
Burned through her blood, and set her afire.
She tried to contain it, but she couldn't name
The light that had sparked this consuming flame.

I looked at what I had written and smiled. By copying the poem and reciting it from memory as I wrote, I could make connections between the sounds of the letters and their words. Between the words and the meaning in some of the lines. It wasn't as though I actually knew when I knew something. Just one day I would realize I understood something that I hadn't understood before. Was this learning?

"Run, Habib! The djinn will get you! Aaar!" Khalid shouted outside the storage room. I sighed. I should get back to work. There was more to do. Always more. I stuffed my notebook back into my trunk and slammed the lid.

Out in the main room, Habib tottered along,

squealing and laughing, while Khalid ran after him with his arms up in the air.

"Boys, please! I'm trying to rest. Just for a little while," Malehkah moaned from where she was trying to relax on a toshak.

Habib made for the front door, but Khalid cut him off. "I'm the djinn! Raaaaa!" Khalid showed his teeth. Habib shouted and ran in a circle toward the back door where they'd come in. "Raaaaaar!" Khalid roared, chasing him with his arms out to the side, flapping them like wings.

Malehkah groaned and flopped a toshak over her head. "Zulaikha, quiet them down! They need a bath anyway. Then wash their clothes too."

When would it stop? When would it get easier? When Malehkah had the baby? When Baba found a husband for me? I touched my whole upper lip and ran my tongue along my teeth. "Now what?" I whispered. My mouth was changed. But every day was the same.

After the boys were bathed and playing quietly, I told Malehkah that I needed to go to the bazaar to buy more soap for the laundry. She didn't even tell me to hurry. She just bit her lower lip and squinted her eyes while she held her belly. When I asked if she was okay, she only told me where the money jar was in the room she shared with Baba. I felt a little guilty for leaving Malehkah all by herself with the boys and with the other work I still needed to do. I'd just have to hurry. Moving quickly and keeping a watch for Anwar, I crossed the river and rushed to the little sewing shop at the end of the bazaar.

"Salaam, child," Meena said as I came into the shop. She put down some curtains she had been sewing. "It is very good to see you again."

In a few minutes, we were sipping our tea back in Meena's little apartment.

"I'm understanding even more of the poem than I did last week when I was here," I said after I took a drink.

"Good," said Meena. She seemed to be looking past me toward the shop.

"Are you expecting someone?"

"What?" She turned her attention back to me. "No. I'm just... That's good, child. You understand more. Very good."

"I'm starting to be able to piece together whole sentences. And learning the sounds in some words can help me figure out other words. It's as if the more I learn, the faster..."

Something was wrong. We'd met many times now, and I'd never quite seen her distracted like this. She wouldn't even meet my gaze. "Muallem-sahib?"

"Hmm?" She looked up and shook her head. "Yes, I'm sorry, Zulaikha. But there's something I've been meaning to discuss with you." She hesitated. "I have been talking to some of my friends. Especially an old friend from Herat, who used to teach at the university there."

I sat up. "How did you meet this person? Was he here?"

"When I heard they were looking for teachers for An Daral's new girls' school, I applied. My friend was visiting. She has a job with the new Department of Education. Imagine my surprise when she interviewed me." Muallem smiled brightly. "And my happiness when they hired me."

"It must have been wonderful to see your old friend," I said.

Muallem nodded. "It's also nice to have a new job. I could use a bit more money." She took a sip of tea and waited for a moment. "I start as soon as the school is built. When that happens, it may be even more difficult to meet for our already rare lessons. So... I spoke to my friend. I told her about you. About your mother. I said that even though you're behind due to a lack of educational opportunities, I believe you could be an extraordinary student."

My cheeks felt hot. "Tashakor, Muallem-sahib."

Meena nodded. She wasn't finished. "Zulaikha, my friend was so impressed by your story that she has offered to teach you, to get you caught up on all the schooling you've missed. You could live and study with her in Herat, and then, when you're ready, maybe you could apply for entrance to the university. Someday you could earn a degree. You could become a teacher at a school like the one here in An Daral, or even at a university in Herat or Kabul. There would be many more options for your future."

I almost dropped my cup, but managed to steady my shaking hand long enough to set it down on the small table. I felt much as I did when Baba told me the Americans could fix my mouth. Only this was something different. To study in Herat? To learn about the great poets in the city where they lived and wrote so long ago? I could hardly imagine how wonderful it would be.

But I was also needed at home. Malehkah would need help with the new baby soon. And with Zeynab gone, there was so much work. And Baba…

"Baba would never let me." I felt like I was rejecting her again the way I had before.

"How do you know?"

"How do I... I mean, I just..."

He had let Najib and me fly all the way to Kandahar for my surgery. And if he was helping to build a new school, maybe he'd be open to girls seeking an education. He'd even encouraged Malehkah to vote. Still, it was a crazy idea. "My family doesn't even know I've been coming to see you. If they find out I've been sneaking around to study here in secret, I'll get a beating. Anyway, even if my father didn't care about any of that, I doubt he'd agree," I said. "It would be too expensive."

Meena smiled. "It's free, child. My friend owes me some favors. And..." She paused. "And I owe your mother this. If it hadn't been for my literature circle..."

I was about to speak again, but Muallem cut in quickly. "Take your time. It is a big decision. Think about it. Ask your father about it. It is a new Afghanistan. Women and girls are back in school, and I think you are destined to be one of them."

I smiled at Meena. She reached out and squeezed my hand. Then she went to her shelf and brought down a worn leather book.

"Now, let's put our thoughts of your bright future to the side for a moment, and turn our attention to the past by looking at more of Firdawsi's *Shahnameh*."

★ ★ ★

When the lesson was finished and I started toward home, I was still thinking about the poems Muallem had showed me. I stopped in the bazaar to buy some peppers for our meal, happy again that my mouth was fixed. Looking normal, I drew much less attention to myself. All around the market, in the café, and just in groups around the street, men were talking about the election.

A young man selling soda in a café waved his hands as he talked. "The Americans rigged the whole thing so this woman... What's her name? This... Malalai Joya would win," he said. "It's not enough that they drop their bombs on our children, now they want their puppets in the capital too!"

An old man with a long white beard twisted the cap off a bottle of orange Zam Zam and nodded. "*Women* don't even want a woman in Parliament. A couple of crazy female ballot-counters changed all the women's votes so Joya would win. My cousin saw this happen."

A third man, in a spotless, bright white perahan-tunban, spoke up. "I cannot believe how you all complain! At least we get to vote. It's better than when the Taliban were in charge."

The shop owner gave the man his change and a hard look. "Tell that to the innocent women and children who the Americans bombed in Kunar Province. They were just trying to dig their families out of the rubble from the first bombing when the Americans hit them again. The Taliban never had bombers."

The man in white shook his head and walked away. "You just can't stand the idea of a woman in Parliament."

A woman in Parliament? Incredible news! Hard to believe. But then, the news about the Americans bombing children was hard to believe too.

"Zulaikha," someone whispered from a narrow alley between two closed-down shops. I jumped at the sound, but it wasn't Anwar. "Zulaikha," she called again.

"Zeynab!" I rushed into the tiny alley and threw my arms around my sister, chadri and all. "Zeynab, is it you?"

She pulled out of my embrace and folded the front of her chadri up over her head so I could see her.

"Zeynab." My hands came to my face as I looked at her. When I last saw my sister, her hair was curled and her face made up. She was radiant. But now there were dark circles under her bloodshot eyes, and her lips were dry and cracked. "What happened?"

"Nothing has happened." She smiled. "Your mouth. So beautiful. I heard that you'd had your surgery. I just wanted to see you."

"What are you doing in An Daral?"

"Tahir is visiting his brother. I managed to convince him to let me come along. We're not staying very long, though."

"Then invite me to your new house. I've missed you so much."

She ran her fingers through her matted, dusty hair. "I wanted to invite you, but I am so very busy. You see, Leena is very nervous and will have one of her attacks if she has to work too hard. Belquis is pregnant and so she can't get around much. Then there are a great many children to take care of. And our house is so big, it…" She bit her finger and turned away for a moment. Then she looked at me and forced a smile "… takes longer to clean," she finished.

"But is your husband kind at least?"

She didn't answer right away, but stared into the distance. Then it was as if she suddenly remembered I had asked her a question. "Yes. Of course he is. I am trying very hard to please him. He is helping to teach me." She moved a lock of hair away from her face and wiped her nose with her chadri. "Every night." She struggled to get her words out. "He wants me to have a son, but I don't know..." She wiped her eyes.

My legs shook. Zeynab had been my whole life. Always so pretty and happy and kind. And now...

I hugged her, squeezing her as she used to squeeze me when I was upset. But now she hung limp in my arms, resting her cheek atop my head. I felt her tears on my chador.

"I will miss you, Zulaikha." She took a step back. "I love you. I always have."

"Wait!" I said. "Don't leave. Come home with me just for a bit. Or we could go someplace and talk." My mind was spinning, dizzy, trying to think of a place we could go.

Zeynab almost smiled. Then she pulled her chadri back down over her face, adjusting it so she could see through the little mesh window. "Khuda hafiz,

Zulaikha." She turned and started walking.

"Wait. Maybe—"

But Zeynab lifted the front hem of her chadri and ran. She had said goodbye, and she meant it.

19

That night at home, I tried to tell Baba that something was wrong with Zeynab, but when he asked me what she'd said that made me so worried, I didn't have a good answer. The problem wasn't in what she said, but in the way she was. We were sisters, and I could tell she was hurting. By the time I tried to explain this, though, Baba had gone back to checking figures on some papers for his business trip to Nimruz Province with Hajji Abdullah.

I spent the next morning and into the afternoon helping him get ready. Malehkah and I packed his clothes and cooked food to put into pots. Baba rushed from the main room of our house to his bedroom and back, checking to make sure he had all the papers he needed.

"Baba-jan?" I asked. He took off the jacket of his Western-style suit, unbuttoned the cuffs on his white shirt, and pushed up his sleeves. He rolled out some construction plans on the window ledge in the main room and mumbled to himself, tracing some of the lines on the paper with his finger. I stepped closer. "Baba?"

He looked up. "Hmm?" He turned back to his papers, shuffling through the stack.

I took a deep breath. I never asked my father for anything, but this would be my last chance to talk to him for weeks. "Baba-jan, if I can get all the housework done early sometime, may I go to visit Zeynab? Maybe Najib could drive me if he catches up on work?"

He didn't answer. Instead, he rolled up the first big paper and flipped through the stack again. "Najibullah!" he yelled. "Go out to the Toyota! Get me my map of Nimruz Province." In a moment, Najib ran out the front door.

"Baba?"

"What?" Baba shouted. "No, you can't go visit Zeynab. Everyone is too busy. Now, you make sure you help Malehkah while I'm away." He smoothed the ridiculous-looking tie. "If I hear that you didn't obey her, I'll be very angry when I get back."

"Bale, Baba," I said, though I thought if I could just get his full attention, I might be able to convince him. I wanted to get him to understand about my

265

encounter with Zeynab in the bazaar. How tired she'd looked. How hollow she'd sounded.

"Will you be gone for a long time, Baba-jan?" Khalid asked.

Baba stood up straight and rubbed the cuff of his shirt over his shiny belt buckle. "Hard to say. The Americans haven't even selected a site for the clinic yet. Then we're required to hire local laborers, and you know what kind of lazy good-for-nothings you'll find down south in Nimruz. After that, we have to stop by Farah City for a few days." He bent down and picked up Habib and Khalid. I wished he would come and hug me too, so that I could talk to him. "We may be gone several weeks. While I'm away, Najibullah is in charge, but you listen to your madar too."

I watched Malehkah huff when Baba-jan slapped Najib on the back. My brother only nodded.

"Baba-jan?" I cut in. "Are you sure I can't—"

"Zulaikha!" Baba shouted. "You are acting like a little baby. Why do you think it is so important to bother me about visiting Zeynab today? Anyway, you said last night that she said that she's fine and her husband is kind."

"But Baba—"

"Enough! I am a busy man and I will not have

my own daughter arguing with me." He squeezed my shoulder. "I'll arrange for you to go see her after I return from my business trip."

My cheeks were hot. "Bale, Baba," I said.

A car horn sounded outside our compound.

"Hajji Abdullah is waiting!" He rolled up the rest of his papers and tied them with string. "Najibullah, help me carry all this to his car." Baba ran out with his papers while Najib carried a trunk containing some of his tools.

"Don't be lazy!" Malehkah snapped at me. She handed me a rolled-up toshak and a sack of food. "Take this out to the compound door so your father and brother don't have to walk so far."

"Bale, Madar." I hoped Najib would be around the house a lot while Baba was gone. I carried the armload of my father's belongings out to the street door. Najib took them from me and handed them to Baba out in the road.

When he came back and locked the door, I heard the car outside pulling away. I'd have to wait a long time to be able to see Zeynab now.

"Zulaikha!" Malehkah shouted from the front porch. "Go to the bazaar and get some rice. When you get back, Torran needs to be milked."

I looked at Najib and my shoulders slumped as I sighed. "Bale, Madar."

My brother frowned at Malehkah. "I'll drive Zulaikha to the bazaar." Najib grinned at me when he saw my smile. He opened the compound gate doors and gave me the same thumbs-up sign he'd given the doctor at Kandahar. "We'll probably be gone a long time. We'll milk Torran when we get back. Or have Khalid do it."

Malehkah stepped forward. "Zulaikha!"

We didn't wait around to hear Malehkah's outrage, but instead climbed into the car. Najib drove down the street, then stopped, reached under his seat, and felt around for something. I felt so free and happy that I clapped my hands. Najib smiled at me. Finally, he pulled out a cassette tape and waved it around. He slipped the tape into the player and then squeezed my arm. Music unlike anything I'd ever heard came on. It wasn't the usual strings, drums, and high-pitched Indian women's voices. Instead, it was a group of men singing in a different language.

"You like?" Najib asked. "I talked to one of the soldiers at Kandahar. He said someone sent him this cassette from America. He says this is *rock and roll*."

I smiled and shrugged. It sounded great. I hardly

ever had the chance to listen to music. We stopped and bought the rice, along with orange Zam Zams and lamb kabobs. Then we just drove around listening to the music, Najib singing loudly in a terrible imitation of English.

After a while, he stopped singing. "I hope you are enjoying your vacation day," he said. He pulled the Toyota onto the road that circled the perimeter yard of the Citadel.

"Why are you taking me along with you?" I asked.

Najib shrugged as he pulled a chunk of lamb off the stick with his teeth. He spoke with his mouth open as he chewed, trying to avoid burning his tongue on the hot food. "When I went with you to Kandahar, it was fun because for a few days I did not have to weld. I thought I would try to pay you back a little."

I smiled. I never knew my older brother was so nice.

"I like your smile," Najib said. "And you do not cover your face any more. This is good. Allah is kind to you."

"Yes," I said. "He is." Najib was talking more on this single ride in the car than I had heard him talk in years. The road wound its way down a little ravine and then up and to the left, bringing us around so that we could see past one of the big towers of the Citadel. "Right after the Americans first came to An Daral, Khalid ran off." I pointed at the wall, tugging my upper lip with my other hand. "I found him halfway up the wall right there and then he got stuck. He was scared. When I climbed up to get him, he nearly fell, and the Citadel police almost caught us."

Najib turned to look at me, his eyebrows raised. "You climbed all the way up there?"

I shrugged. "What else could I do? Malehkah would have been furious with me if I let Khalid fall."

We laughed at my mean little joke. Then Najib turned the car away from the Citadel. "I want to show you something," he said. He drove back down the hill, winding among the walls of An Daral until we had passed the last compound on the east side of town.

"Where are we going?" I asked.

"You'll see." He drove the Toyota up a long, winding road, over bumps and ruts, until finally we turned out onto a little flat place partway up the mountain. Then he pulled the lever up between our seats and shut off the engine.

Ahead of us, down below, all of An Daral lay stretched out with its streets and houses. And above it all, in the distance, rose the high walls of the ancient Citadel.

"It's beautiful here," I said. "Like flying."

"I used to sneak up here when I was a boy. Whenever I could get away." Najib spoke slowly and quietly, looking straight out the windshield. "I mean, before I started working. Now all I do is weld."

I frowned and turned toward my brother. "Don't you like welding?"

Najib took a deep breath. "Does it matter? Since I was ten years old, and for the rest of my life, that's what I'll do. That's who I'll be. Najibullah the welder."

He sounded so sad. I wanted to put my arm around him. "But you and Baba-jan are making more money. The business is doing well."

He smiled at me. "It is. Praise Allah. We are doing very well. Only, when I was with you in Kandahar, I saw all these soldiers. Not just regular Americans either. Americans from China, Africa, everywhere. And they weren't just fighter soldiers. There were doctor soldiers. Computer soldiers. Mechanic soldiers."

"You want to join the army?"

He chuckled a little. "No! no, I could never do that. Only I wonder sometimes what I might have done if Baba had not made me a welder."

"Sometimes I wonder what I might do with my life," I said. He folded his hands in his lap and waited for me to continue. I told him everything. I told him all about Meena and the poetry and about trying to learn to read and write. Then, although I almost lost my courage to keep going, I even told him about the school in Herat.

"That's wonderful! Did you ask Baba about it?"

"How could I?" I said. "It's a crazy idea anyway. He'll probably say no."

"But you said the school would be free?"

I nodded.

Najib clapped his hands. "Baba will say yes. I know he will. He'll be so happy when this Nimruz project pays off that he'll agree to anything."

"You think so? It just feels like an impossible dream."

"Zulaikha, people used to say the same thing about you having your mouth fixed. I would have said that about flying in a helicopter to an army base in Kandahar. It's like Baba always says, these are good times. A new Afghanistan!"

"I don't know," I said, but I couldn't hold back my smile.

"*I* know. We'll talk to Baba together when he returns. If he can be convinced to get you your surgery, he'll agree to let you go to a good Herat school."

"Bale, Najib!" I practically squealed as I squeezed his arm.

My brother started the engine and turned the car around. "And we'll make sure to invite Zeynab back home to visit us too!" Then he turned the music up loud and we both sang along in our own made-up English. It was one of the happiest afternoons I could remember.

We pulled up outside our compound as the sun was setting. Najib honked the horn and waited for Malehkah or Khalid to open the big double car doors. He waited and then held down the horn button longer.

After the third horn blast, the doors swung open and Najib drove the car in. He shut off the motor and both of us climbed out as Malehkah closed the doors behind us. Waiting for her angry words, I stepped around the car, but instead I heard only her sniffling. She wiped tears from her eyes. We'd hurt her feelings, leaving her like that.

Somehow, even after all she had done to me, I felt

bad for her. "Malehkah," I said. "I'm sorry we—"

"Zeynab has been burned. They came with the news maybe twenty minutes after you left. I sent Khalid out to find you, but…" She struggled to speak. "They say it's pretty bad."

I couldn't move. I wanted to scream, but I couldn't breathe.

"Where?" Najib asked.

"All over her body."

"Where is she?" Najib shouted.

Malehkah took a step back. "At the hospital in Farah."

Najib ran to the corner of the compound and grabbed a big white plastic jug. He opened the gas cap and stuck in a plastic funnel. But even with that, his shaking hands still spilled some fuel. After a few minutes, when gas overflowed and splashed back out, Najib cursed. "Get me a wet rag!" he snapped. He dumped the extra gas on the ground. When Malehkah returned with a dripping cloth, Najib washed his hands the best he could before running around to the driver's seat.

I rushed forward to the passenger side. Malehkah grabbed me as I opened the door. "Zulaikha, you should—"

"She's my *sister*!" I slapped her hand away and slammed the door closed behind me. The motor was already running and Najib leaned against the horn, screaming curses at Malehkah to open the door.

"Najib?" I asked. He didn't answer, backing the car out of the compound before driving off down our street. "Najib?"

"Be quiet!" He leaned forward, staring carefully ahead as he drove the car faster and faster, spinning the back wheels out in loose rocks on some curves, slamming the brakes when we came upon a deep rut in the road. Every time he had to slow down, he cursed or hit his fist down on the dashboard.

I rubbed my hands together and then put them over my face. My legs shook. The afternoon's kabob wanted to come back up.

Zeynab was burned. What did that mean? How was she burned? What happened?

"Maybe it's not so bad," I said. Then the tears came.

20

We reached Farah City in far less time than it had taken before. Najib asked for directions to the hospital as soon as we got to town. He brought the car skidding to a stop outside the hospital gate. Night had fallen.

A guard rushed out of the gatehouse. He pointed his rifle at us. "Slow down! What's your hurry?"

"My sister," Najib shouted out his window. "She's been burned. They say she's here."

"Well, you're not driving that fast in here!"

"Bale," Najib said. He drummed his fingers on the steering wheel.

The guard pulled the gate open and Najib drove inside. The front courtyard was mostly gravel for parking, but there were several large, dried-out flower beds. Not even weeds grew in them. Tall trees formed a sort of canopy that drenched the place in gloom. When the wind stirred the branches, little jagged shadows cut the moonlight along the ground. It would have been pretty, if it weren't such a horrible place.

We stepped out of the car. Smoke billowed from under the hood. A group of men sat on the cement front porch. The red-orange lights from their cigarettes flared in the dark, and the conversation quieted as we approached.

"You tear your car up driving so fast." Tahir drew a long drag on his cigarette and stood up.

"Tahir, sahib." Najib addressed Zeynab's husband in tight, controlled words. "What happened?"

"Nobody knows." Tahir shrugged. "There was an accident. A hose must have come loose on the cookstove when she was making supper. She caught on fire." He blew out a big puff of smoke. "But we put it out quickly. She'll be fine." Najib nodded and we turned to go into the building, but Tahir grabbed my brother by the shirt. "Whoa, rafiq. She is in the women's section of the hospital. You cannot go in there."

I didn't even wait for Najib's approval. I ran inside, letting the wooden screen door slam shut behind me. Blinking from my tears and from the light as I came in out of the dark, I was horrified at the sight of the filthy place. The bare cement floor needed to be swept. The single light in the middle of the hallway barely prevented total darkness, but still attracted a frantic swarm of flying bugs. I called out to the first person I saw. He was at the end of the dingy hallway, looking at some papers. "My sister Zeynab was burned. Where is she?"

The man looked up with a frown. "Are you a visitor here? Did you check in with the hospital administrator?"

"What?" I couldn't believe this man was going to bother with procedure in this disgusting, run-down place. "Let me see my sister!"

The man sighed, shook his head, and then gestured for me to follow him down the hall. A door was open to the night, without even a screen. In the next dark room, a horrible rotting smell stung my nose. The man pulled a string to turn on the light. Next to a large empty washtub, blankets stained in blood or waste made a feast for the buzzing flies.

This was a hospital? They had brought my sister to this place to get better?

The man led me past the laundry and stopped outside an open door, motioning me into a chamber lit only by a dim lamp in the corner. I went inside. From across the room, I saw my sister in the only bed. She didn't look so bad. She was wearing her pretty dress with the pink and purple flowers.

I slowly stepped closer.

"Oh, Allah, have mercy," I whispered. "Zeynab."

She wasn't wearing a dress. She wasn't wearing anything except a stained white sheet over her legs. The beautiful pink and purple flowers weren't flowers at all, not beautiful at all. It was her scorched and blistered skin.

"Oh." I looked at her. I shifted my weight from one foot to another. "Oh, Zeynab. Oh."

My sister lay naked from the waist up, moaning softly. She was burned everywhere, all over her body. The top layers of her skin had somehow shrunk back, tearing into clumps that had then bubbled and blistered into a dark purple-black. The exposed skin below was bright pink. A section of the skin over her stomach had scorched to a sort of yellow and peeled back. Her breasts were bright pink, her nipples bits of black char. Her neck was a bleeding, oozing black wound.

But the worst was her face. I sobbed almost to a scream. Her beautiful, long, dark hair looked as if it had melted into her seared scalp. Her nose had disappeared almost completely. There were no lashes on her closed eyes. Her eyebrows were gone.

And her mouth, her lips that had never been

horrible like mine, were twisted and cracked. Her upper lip had split in the middle, rolling back to expose her teeth. All my life, I had wished and prayed to be like my sister. To have a pretty face and a normal mouth. I never ever, not for one second, wanted her to look like I used to.

"Zeynab," I wailed. "Zeynab." Was she dead? I did my best to stop sniffling and lowered my ear over her mouth. The smell assaulted my nose – a horrible salty-sweet-sour smell, like the worst stench from the butcher district on the hottest day – and I clamped my hand to my mouth as I gagged. But she was breathing. She was still alive.

I fell into a chair beside my sister's bed, almost dizzy. "Zeynab," I cried. "Zeynab. Zeynab."

I don't know how much time passed before I felt the hand on my shoulder, but it startled me so much that I sprang up and spun around.

"Zulaikha." It was Captain Mindy and Shiaraqa. Next to them by the hallway door was Corporal Andrews. He looked at me and nodded. Seeing him so serious, where before he had always been smiling and happy, brought fresh tears to my eyes.

"Why are you here?" Shiaraqa asked.

I wiped my eyes. "My sister."

Shiaraqa told the captain what I had said and she gasped, covering her mouth. For a moment, I wondered how Shiaraqa and Corporal could be in the women's wing, but then I sobbed. The Americans with their stupid guns could do whatever they wanted. Anyway, it didn't matter. They weren't looking at my sister in a bad way. How could they? How could anyone look at her that way ever again?

I took a deep breath to try to collect myself, and a heavy smell hit my nose. It was Zeynab on the bed next to me, her eyes open, staring at the ceiling. She did not speak.

"Zulaikha, are you okay?" It was Shiaraqa who spoke, translating again for the captain.

Of course I was okay. It was my sister who was... who was...

"Can you help her?" I asked, speaking directly to Captain Mindy as though she could understand.

When she heard the translation, she wiped a tear from her eye and blinked several times. Shiaraqa translated her words. "Captain Edmanton is very sorry about what happened to your sister. She says the Farah Hospital doctors called for American help. She has radioed the American base at Kandahar and asked them to send a helicopter so that your sister can be flown to the good doctors there. They are waiting for an answer. She wants to try to help her the best she can."

Captain Mindy opened a bag that she had brought with her. She took out a small wet white cloth and rubbed it on Zeynab's arm. Then she pulled out a clear bag with a tube and prepared a needle. Once the needle was in my sister's arm, she taped it down before turning to me. "This will help her feel a little better until we can get her to a good hospital," Shiaraqa translated. "She says there is not much else we can do for her in this place."

Captain Mindy knelt down in front of me and took hold of my shoulders. She looked into my eyes and said something to Corporal Andrews. In a moment, he handed me a plastic bottle of cool water. The captain helped me tip the bottle to my lips and I drank. Then she ran her hand over my hair and spoke. Shiaraqa translated. "If we move her to a good hospital quickly, there is a chance we can save her."

"Zul... aikha." It was Zeynab, speaking in short hisses. I rushed to her side, leaning over her to hear her better. Her eyes, thank Allah, were not burned. When she saw me, her smile turned into a wince as the hot skin at the corners of her mouth cracked and bled.

The captain said through Shiaraqa, "Tell her she must not try to speak. She must rest. A helicopter should be on the way to take her to get help."

My sister turned her eyes, not her head, to see who was there. She seemed to focus in on Shiaraqa for a moment before her gaze returned to the ceiling. "No," she whispered.

"What, Zeynab?"

"Zulaikha," Captain Mindy said softly.

I ignored her. "What did you say, Zeynab?"

The captain put her hand on my shoulder. "Zulaikha—"

"She is *my* sister and she wants to talk to me!" I yelled. Captain Mindy looked at Shiaraqa for the translation, but he only shook his head.

A tear streamed back from Zeynab's eye and she groaned in pain. It must have burned on her scorched face. "No," she whispered. "No… fly. Let… me… mmmmm…" Her eyes rolled in her head as she trembled. "Let… me… die."

Die? My Zeynab? Oh, no. A thousand times no. "Zeynab, they can help you. The Americans can fix you the way they fixed my mouth."

The radio that Captain Mindy had clipped to her chest squawked and a loud voice spoke over it. She quickly covered it and stepped out into the hallway.

"Let… me… die," said Zeynab. Each word was a quiet, forced wheeze.

"Oh, no, please, Zeynab," I cried.

Captain Mindy stepped back into the room and spoke firmly to Shiaraqa. I looked to him and he translated. "A helicopter is on its way. She needs to know if your sister takes any medicine."

I asked Zeynab and she whispered no.

Shiaraqa spoke more quietly. "Is she pregnant?"

Zeynab heard the question and painful tears sprang from her eyes. "No," she whispered in little gasps. "He say… He… say…" She winced against the pain. "He say… I… can't."

Shiaraqa nodded and left the room. My eyes went wide and I put a hand to my open mouth. "But it's only been a few months," I said. Without thinking about my words, I added, "You can still have a baby. You will, Zeynab. Think about your little boy. He'll be so beautiful."

Zeynab shuddered as more tears burned her face. After a few quiet but tense moments, Shiaraqa rushed back into the room and spoke to Captain Mindy.

She looked at him and answered in rapid English, punching her fist into her hand. He answered and the Captain threw her hands up and shook her head.

"What is the problem?" I asked.

Shiaraqa would not even face me. When he spoke, he looked at the captain. "Your sister's husband says he cannot afford to stay with her in Kandahar through her treatment, and that his wives may not go without their husband as an escort. He says the Americans should treat your sister here in Farah."

How could Tahir say such a thing? Didn't he understand how serious Zeynab's burns were? He was a rich man. He could afford the time away from work to go to Kandahar. He had to know that this hospital was nothing like an American hospital. This place was dirty. The people here hadn't run one tube into her arm as the Americans had. They hadn't even bandaged Zeynab. She was simply lying there on the bed.

Mercifully, Zeynab was asleep again. Over the next few hours, Captain Mindy and Shiaraqa went outside several times. I knew they were arguing with Tahir. Every time they came back, the captain was angrier. I looked down at Zeynab's charred and peeled-away skin. My sweet sister was dying.

She was dying and her husband, Tahir, didn't care.

Everything blurred in my tears. I stood there, remembering how beautiful and wonderful Zeynab had been, my strength and friend and hope through my whole life. I stood there, watching her suffer, listening to her raspy, shallow breathing. I stood there until just before the dawn, when finally she breathed no more.

In the murky mix between yesterday and today, between light and dark, I squeezed Zeynab's hand for the last time. I should have cried. I should have screamed and pulled out my hair. But I had shed all the tears I had left. I was exhausted and dizzy from a long, long night in this horrible, hot room. I pulled the white sheet up to cover my sister. Then I turned away.

There was nothing more to be done here. Zeynab's dead body, just like her life, belonged to Tahir now. I stepped out of the room. The only light spilled in through an open door at the end of the hallway near the front of the hospital.

"Zulaikha?" Captain Mindy said as I passed. She put her hand on my arm but I pulled away, staggering toward the front door.

I hadn't realized how thick the heat had been in

the hospital until I was outside on the front porch and the cool air stung my face.

Najib sprang to his feet. "Zeynab?"

I only shook my head. I couldn't say the word. Najib turned away quickly and I took his hand.

We passed Tahir, who stood up, yawning and stretching. He didn't shed a single tear. I was too sad, too tired to be shocked. My sister was only one of his wives. He had two others. He was a rich man and could marry again.

Shiaraqa called after me, translating something Captain Mindy was saying, but I kept walking with my brother to the car. Only when Najib was in the driver seat did I turn around and see Shiaraqa hadn't been calling after me at all. Instead, he was speaking in a loud voice to Captain Mindy. The captain shouted, pointed at Shiaraqa, and then pointed at Tahir. When Shiaraqa shook his head and responded in English again, Captain Mindy grabbed his perahan-tunban and shook him. Finally, Shiaraqa nodded and turned to Tahir.

"What does this crazy woman want?" Tahir asked.

"She says she thinks you're wrong to be so old and marry so young a girl."

"She doesn't understand. She knows nothing. These things happen." Tahir shrugged. "Anyway, why does she care so much for this one girl when the Americans have killed thousands? Tell this little tramp to go on home." He took a step toward the captain. I heard a metallic click and saw Corporal Andrews standing closer to them both, his rifle ready and his finger on the trigger.

Tahir's chest heaved up and down as he breathed deep. He looked at the captain and then at the corporal. Taking a step back, he held up his empty, thick, sausage-finger hands. He spoke softly to Shiaraqa. "This is how the Americans do everything, bossing everyone around with their big guns, pretending to be heroes because they act like they care for one girl who burned in an accident."

The captain erupted into English, her words blurring together in an angry rush. She motioned for Shiaraqa to translate, but didn't pause to let him catch up.

"She says... you're a very bad man." Shiaraqa sounded uncertain. Captain Mindy's shouting got even louder and she held up her fist. Shiaraqa's eyes widened. "A very, very bad man."

Finally, the captain spat at Tahir's feet as she

stepped past him. Corporal Andrews kept watching him with his gun ready. The captain ran to me and crouched down beside me. When she pulled me in close to hug me, I didn't resist her. It all felt unreal, like she wasn't hugging me, but some other girl I was watching in a nightmare that would never end.

She let me go, and I looked at her for a moment before I got into the car.

My brother Najibullah wept all the way home.

21

The month following Zeynab's death was long and painful.

Hajji Abdullah's family reached Baba by satellite phone, and he came home late the day my sister died. He looked drained and empty. Hollow, the way I felt. I never saw him cry, not even at her funeral, but he locked himself in his room for days. I'd take him food sometimes. Other times Malehkah or Najib would try to get him to eat. Either way, he did not eat much.

When he finally did come out, he still didn't talk. He just went back to work, building the clinic in Nimruz and welding at the base in Farah. He was even working with the Abdullahs, trying to get the contract to improve the old Russian air base that the Americans were using to the north in Shindand. Baba was a busy man.

Malehkah's baby came. We did not celebrate as people usually did when a new baby was born. It was a girl. We named her Safia. She cried at night sometimes. I half wondered if she was crying over Zeynab like I was. A few days after she was born, Malehkah was better able to help with the work around the compound.

"Zulaikha, when you're finished dusting, will you sort the rice for dinner?" Malehkah stood in the doorway to the storage room, holding the new baby. Lately, she actually asked me to do chores, instead of ordering me as she had always done.

"I've sorted it already, Madar."

"Ah. Feed Torran then."

"I've done that too."

"Bale." She left the room.

That was how most of our exchanges had been lately. Except for the baby's cries, the house had been quiet. I launched myself into chores, and when those were done, I sneaked away alone to practice my writing. Maybe I worked so hard because it helped to keep my mind focused on something. Maybe I volunteered for all those chores because when I did them, I didn't have to focus my mind at all.

I wiped the sweat from my upper lip, then shook my head. Everything was supposed to be perfect once my mouth was fixed. Zeynab was supposed to be happily married. I was supposed to marry his handsome brother. The two of us would raise our children together. But nothing had happened the way it was supposed to. Maybe I looked normal. Maybe even a little pretty. What difference did it make? What had beauty done for Zeynab? I felt the tears coming, and so I bit my lower lip. I could do that now, with my new mouth. I did that a lot.

I pulled my notebook from my trunk and slipped it into the pocket of my dress. Malehkah was in the kitchen, humming and peeling potatoes while Safia slept in a basket.

"Do you need anything from the bazaar?" I asked.

"Onions." Malehkah pulled a stack of bills out of her pocket and counted off fifty Afghanis.

As I went through the courtyard, Khalid came out of his fort behind the fuel drums in the front corner of the compound. Habib was with him. "Buy us some candy?" I nodded to them on my way out.

Outside, a dog barked in the distance and a gentle breeze blew a dried-up leaf across the dirt road. The water in the river was cold. Soon I'd need to wear shoes when I crossed.

In the bazaar, I bought three onions. I didn't even argue about the price. I'd give the boys some of what was left of the candy the Americans had given me.

When I had rounded the corner from the bazaar road and passed a few compounds down Meena's street, Anwar and Salman came out of a side alley, laughing, pushing, and shoving each other. As soon as Anwar saw me, his smile vanished and he held up his arm to stop his cousin. I clenched my fists at my side. My stomach felt like it was twisting over.

"Look, Anwar," said Salman. "It's Zulaikha with her pretty new mouth."

I wheeled around in the direction I had come, but Anwar rushed to block my way. They had me cut off from the bazaar and from home. My legs felt wobbly again, almost as bad as that morning they had cornered me on the river road.

"Naw, look at that scar," Anwar said. "Don't let her fool you. She's just the same old Donkeyface." He put his fingers straight out from under his nose to imitate the way my teeth used to be.

Used to be. I didn't look at all the same any more. I didn't feel the same any more. Couldn't they think of new mean things to say? How could they still think this was funny?

"HEEEE-HAAAAAW," Salman droned. Anwar slapped his cousin on the back and laughed.

The same old jokes every time, and now the insults weren't even true. I stood and simply watched the boys laugh at me. They could do what they wanted. I couldn't make myself care.

Anwar frowned, as though he sensed that something besides my mouth was different from the last time we'd been through this. He pulled back his fist. Suddenly, he lurched forward like he was going to hit me. I flinched when his fist came close.

But he didn't hit me. He stopped his fist a few centimeters back. He grinned at Salman and then at me. "Just testing," he said.

All the same as that day on the river road. He hadn't really hit me. He'd stopped short. The only difference was that back then, his hateful words had hurt, because I did look horrible.

"The way I look doesn't make a difference," I said. "Nothing does."

"What are you talking about, Donkeyface?" Salman shouted.

"It never made a difference, except that the insults and the threats used to bother me." It was time to forget about what these boys were always saying, about what they would always say, no matter what happened. "Khuda hafiz, Anwar." I stepped past Anwar and Salman and went on my way to Meena's shop.

"Wait a minute!" Anwar shouted, rushing to block my path again. "I didn't give you permission to leave yet!"

I faked to the right and then stepped around Anwar to the left. "I've given myself permission."

"Donkeyface, where you going?" Salman said.

I didn't reply. I kept walking. Anwar caught up with me.

"I can still see the scar, Zulaikha. You're still ugly," he said. "You'll always have the scars."

At another time I might have smiled. These boys I had always been so afraid of, they were powerless except to call me mean names. They weren't going to do anything to me. I walked right past them.

"Aw, who cares about old ugly Donkeyface?" Anwar said from somewhere behind me.

I forced myself not to look back. When I reached Meena's shop, I finally turned to check behind me. The street was empty. Anwar and Salman were gone.

Meena welcomed me in as always. She put on the tea and we took our usual seats. I didn't say anything, but handed her my notebook.

She examined the pages I had copied. "Good." She turned more pages. "Very good."

I wished I could enjoy her praise. She must have noticed something in my expression when she looked up from my work. "But how are you, child?"

"I..." The tightness was back in my throat. "I can't stop thinking about Zeynab."

"Nor should you, Zulaikha." Muallem's voice was very quiet.

"She was so beautiful and..." I bit my lower lip. "I mean, I always thought if I could be even a small part as pretty as my sister..." Then the tears came. "I miss her. It just hurts so much."

Meena stood up and went for the tea. She placed my cup on the table next to me and poured. "'Every triumph from patience springs, the happy herald of better things.'"

"But what better things?" I wiped my nose with my chador. Meena poured a cup for herself and then sat down. She watched me through the steam over her cup and said nothing. I took a sip. "You mean the school? In Herat?"

"I did not say so, child. You must decide for yourself if that's the desire Allah has placed in your heart." She lowered her cup and held it with both hands in her lap. "I will help you no matter what you decide, but I cannot make the decision for you."

"The poems you have me copying," I said. "They make more sense. In the back of my notebook, I started to write a letter… to Zeynab, and to my madar-jan." I rubbed the tears from my eyes. "You can check it over if you—"

"No." Meena leaned back on her bed. "No, those are sacred words, between you and your mother and sister." She closed her eyes and rested her head against the wall. "You're learning. You are a very good student."

"The poems are the only things that bring me peace. Poems and prayer. They comfort me." I stopped and waited for Meena to say something, but she only nodded, her eyes still closed. "But I can't go to Herat," I said. She didn't move. "Baba would never let me."

Meena kept her eyes closed but raised her eyebrows. "Really, child? Have you asked him?"

"I'm too afraid to," I said, looking down. "He's… He's not the same since Zeynab died. And he'd be furious to know I've been sneaking away from the house and coming here. And…" I sighed. "I worry that if he finds out I've been learning, he'll put a stop to it." This time my teacher was quiet for so long that I wondered if she was sleeping. "Anyway, 'every triumph from patience springs,' right?"

Now Muallem's eyes were wide open. She was more awake than I had ever seen her. "Haven't you been patient long enough?" She gestured at herself and then at me. "Haven't we all waited long enough?" She leaned toward me. "What if this chance for school is the better thing that you were always destined to be patient for?"

"Herat isn't going anywhere."

Muallem nodded. "Yes. But as we get older, as we gain more responsibilities, life's options have the tendency to slip away."

I breathed in deeply and huffed out over the steam from my tea. "I have to do this now, don't I?"

"Of course not, child. But it may be much more difficult to do later. Not that convincing your father to allow you to go to Herat for your studies will be easy now."

"But it would be worth it," I said, to myself as much as Meena.

As if by unspoken agreement, we fell into our work, reviewing some of the poems we'd read before and practicing new words. When it was time to go,

Muallem gave me a new page of poetry to copy. I picked up my bag of onions from the bazaar and went through the shop to the street door.

"Muallem-sahib?" I asked as I reached the door. She looked up at me. "Do you pray?"

"Absolutely, child. It seems I hardly ever stop praying."

I smiled. "Will you pray for me tonight?"

Meena made a little bow. "Bale, Zulaikha."

22

That night, we ate much later than usual because Baba and Najib arrived home late from work. When we were all seated around the dastarkhan, I stared at my rice and naan and twisted my old dinner towel in my lap. I no longer needed it as I did before my surgery, but right then I found it comforting.

"We should be finished with the clinic in a few weeks. The Americans have inspected our progress and they are very impressed." Baba spoke plainly, with some of his old excitement. "They paid me the third installment of my total payment, and they say that if I finish before the end of the month, which I easily will, they will give me a hundred thousand Afghani bonus. Can you believe that?"

Baba tore off a piece of naan with his teeth. "What did I tell you, Najibullah? You watch your workers carefully or they will work slowly, sleep on the job if they can. Watch them, work with them now and then so they will like you and work harder for you. Then…" He pointed at Najib. "… Then you will get results."

Baba wasn't exactly happy, but he was in a better mood than I'd seen him in for a long time. This was good. It was a good time to ask him about Herat. But how could I, when he would hardly stop talking about his jobs and his money? My palms were sweaty and my hands shook. Finally, I jumped in and spoke up. "Baba-jan, I need—"

"Yes, I know." He smiled at me. I had not expected this kind of happy reaction. "I know. You need new clothes. A few new dresses. Some shoes." His eyes narrowed and he tilted his head to look at me. "Maybe it is even time to get you a chadri."

Clearly Baba was thinking about other things for me. Maybe I should wait. I took a drink of water. Or maybe Meena was right and I had waited long enough.

"Baba-jan," I said. My stomach felt so twisted I worried I would lose my food. Maybe I should let it go. It would be enough just to learn from Meena.

"What, Zulaikha?" said Baba.

I lowered my eyes. "Nothing."

"Come on, Zulaikha. What troubles you? There's nothing your baba can't fix."

When I started talking next, I was surprised at how fast the words spilled out. "I've been meeting with a woman, a muallem who used to teach in Herat and who was friends with Madar-jan. She's been teaching me to read and write. She has a friend who teaches at the university in Herat now. This friend has offered to let me live and study with her... that is, with your permission... until one day I'm ready to apply to the university."

It was all out. Nobody in the room moved. I risked a look at Baba to see if he had heard me. He dropped the chicken he'd been eating right into the rice bowl.

I went on quickly so I wouldn't lose him. "It wouldn't cost anything. Meena said—"

Baba's eyes went wide. "Meena?" He half whispered the name. "Meena." Did he know her? Maybe he remembered her from years ago.

Too late to stop now. "It's just that I have already learned a lot and—"

"You aren't going to Herat." Baba spoke with his mouth packed full of chicken. He stared off into the distance for a moment. Finally, he shook his head and pointed at me with a scowl. "And if I hear about you meeting with that Meena woman again, I'll beat you myself."

I bit my lower lip and twisted the towel in my lap. Nobody spoke.

My father let out a little chuckle. "What would you need school for anyway? You're already learning all you need at the school of Malehkah." He turned to his wife. "Right?" But she did not smile back at him, or even look away as she usually did. When he saw that I didn't smile either, he stopped laughing himself. He swallowed and wiped his mouth with the back of his hand. "Why do you waste my time with these stupid ideas?"

That was his answer then. It was over. I should have known. Everybody went back to eating in silence. I ate a pinch of rice.

What would my madar-jan have done? She never gave up on her studies even when the Taliban outlawed her books. It had been *that* important to her. And she'd made me promise to do all I could to learn as much as possible. I owed it to her, and to Meena, and to Zeynab. "Meena doesn't think it's stupid," I said. "She has already arranged for my school and for a place with a respected Afghan woman. She said Madar-jan used to—"

"I said no!" My father sprang to his feet. "You see?" he shouted. He pointed at Najib. "Remember this, Najibullah. This is what happens when you are too soft on women. The Americans let their women boss them around like they own everything. Then you offer your daughter some nice clothes and what does she do?" He turned to me. "She spits it back in your face and disrespects you in your own house!"

Little baby Safia jolted awake at the sudden noise. Khalid looked surprised. He reached for Habib, who was crying, and led him out the back door by the hand.

I stood up. "Please, Baba-jan—"

"You call me jan? Like you hold me dear when you just told me what a stupid, backward Afghan I am?" He kicked the bowl of rice, scattering food across the room. "This is all because of ideas put in your head by that American whore!"

I bit my lower lip. "I just want to learn. I just want a chance. I can make you proud of me, Baba—"

"You'll make me proud, all right! When you're good and married off. But you're not going to school, especially not in Herat! My word is final and I won't—"

"Let her go to the school." Malehkah had taken the crying baby into the kitchen and come back. She stood up straight, a few paces behind my father.

Baba's nose wrinkled into a snarl. He did not look at his wife. "What did you say, Malehkah?"

"If she wants to go to the school and the school is paid for, let her go. You've already lost one daughter. Do you want to lose—"

Baba swung his arm back and struck Malehkah with the back of his big fist. She flew backward to the floor and landed hard, her head hitting the cement. My father took a step toward me, but before he could take another, Najib stood in front of me.

"Baba, enough," he said.

My father stared with his mouth open. He held his hand up in front of his face, wet with his wife's blood on his new gold rings. In a moment, tears fell.

"I..." he whispered. "I loved Zeynab. I love..." He turned and looked at Malehkah. If the blood from her nose hadn't bubbled when she breathed, I would have thought she was dead. He turned back to me and wiped at his tears, smearing blood on his face. Then he ran out the front door.

Outside, the street door slammed shut. Najib faced me. He was shaking and his shoulders rose and fell in heavy breaths.

"Go." I motioned to the door. "Go with Baba. I'll help Malehkah and the kids."

My brother nodded and left. I poured some water on my old dinner towel and then sat down next to Malehkah, wiping her forehead and then wiping the blood from her face. "Come on, Madar-jan. It's okay. You're safe now." I propped her head up on my lap and smoothed her hair with my fingers.

Khalid peeked in around the corner of the door from outside. "Is Baba still mad?"

I looked up and held out my hand to him. "No, bacha. Everything's okay. You and Habib come on inside now." I gently cleaned the rest of Malehkah's face and then hugged both boys when they crouched down beside me.

Habib pointed to his mother. "Madar?"

Tears rolled down Khalid's face. How different he looked now from when he was angry and calling me hateful names. Now he was only helpless and scared. I hugged him again. He was growing and changing, and would only continue to do so, but he'd always be my little brother.

Finally, Malehkah opened her eyes. She touched her nose and groaned in pain. Then she looked up at me and realized she was lying in my lap.

"Help me to the kitchen," she said. "Will you hand me Safia? She'll be hungry."

"Bale, Madar," I said. After I helped Malehkah settle down on the floor of the kitchen, I let the boys snuggle in close to her. Then I carefully picked up my tiny baby sister, who had cried herself to sleep. She opened her eyes and yawned with her little pink face. "It's okay, Safia. You're okay." I gently eased her into Malehkah's waiting arms.

I watched as Malehkah put the little mouth to her breast. The baby drank and drank. Malehkah closed her eyes, her nose already crooked and swollen in shades of black and blue.

"I've got to get dinner cleaned up," she whispered. "We don't want bugs."

"I'll take care of it, Madar. Just rest. Please."

"Tashakor, Zulaikha," she said.

I turned to Khalid. "Khalid-jan, could you help Madar and me? Could you go out to the well and draw a bucket of water so that we can wash up from dinner?"

Khalid rubbed his eyes and turned back to bury his face against his mother's shoulder.

"Khalid," Malehkah said.

"It's okay, Madar. I'll take care of it. All of you just rest."

I went out into the dark back courtyard and set

my bucket down next to the well while I pulled up a full pail of water. I could hear them talking inside. The different and varied tones of my brothers. The muffled sound of Malehkah's tired voice, trying to calm her children.

I filled my bucket and took the water inside. While it heated on the stove, I helped get Habib and Khalid settled in to sleep. Then there were dishes to clear and the floor to sweep. When I returned to the kitchen to wash the pots, I found Malehkah standing, wobbling on shaky feet.

"Madar, please lie back down!" I hurried to her side, took her arm, and eased her back to the floor.

"I thought I would help," said Malehkah. She gently put her hand to her face and turned to me. "I'm glad you found Meena. That's why I sent you on all those extra trips to the bazaar."

"You knew?" All my life it seemed that Malehkah complained about everything I did. It seemed impossible that she had been trying to help me go to my lessons all along. Though yesterday I would have said a lot of what had happened tonight was impossible. "Madar, if you knew I was studying with Meena, why did you—"

"I'm just so dizzy. Head hurts."

When she was resting on the floor again, I put a damp towel over her forehead. "Tashakor, Madar-jan."

It took a few hours to wash, dry, and put away all the dishes. By the time I had done that and checked on the kids, Malehkah had fallen asleep. I sat down, leaning against the wall in the kitchen, where I stayed by her side through the long night.

I jumped awake at the sound of the front house door squeaking on its bad hinge. I stood and looked through the little kitchen window. The dark sky was just beginning to take on the first hints of morning light. Soon the muezzin would call the faithful to prayer. I whispered to Malehkah, "Stay here." As I moved to see who had come in, the door to the kitchen opened. Baba stood in the doorway with Najib right behind him. My father rubbed his knuckles against his rough, unshaven chin. He watched Malehkah and me for a long time.

Najib gently squeezed his elbow. "Go ahead, Baba-jan. You can do it. It's just like we talked about."

Baba nodded. He took one step into the kitchen. "I..." He swallowed and licked his lips. "I've been working this over in my mind. All night." He slid his hands down his face. "Malehkah, please forgive me.

I should not have hit you so hard." My father stopped for a moment, and then went on. "Your mother, Zulaikha. You were too young to remember, but your mother loved her books. Always with her it was these old Afghan poets." A small shudder went through him, and he bit his lower lip as he struggled to regain control of his wavering voice. "They... they killed her for those books."

"But the Taliban—"

My father held up a hand. Malehkah tugged on my skirt from where she sat.

"They killed her. They should have killed me. Or I should have stopped them." A single tear rolled down my father's cheek. He did not try to hide it. "I... I've been thinking. This school you've been talking about." He shrugged. "They say the educated ones make all the money. But what do I know?" He waved his fingers in a circle in front of his face, as though he had much more to say but couldn't squeeze out the words. As though he were struggling for air. "It's a new Afghanistan, right? I'm just an illiterate welder. I just—"

"I don't want to go to Herat," I said. It is what I had realized as I took care of Malehkah, the boys, and the baby during the night. My father frowned, and I continued. "I love my family too much. I can't abandon them. I'm needed here."

"Zulaikha," Malehkah said.

Baba began, "Last night you said—"

"I do want to go to school, Baba-jan. I want to learn. I need to go to school." Before last night I could never have believed I would be saying this today. "But my family needs me too. The kids are small and Madar is overworked. I can't abandon them." I took a deep breath. "So I was hoping that I could go to school here in An Daral, at the school you helped build. I hear they've hired a very good teacher there." I held my breath, waiting for my father's reply, afraid and excited at the same time. But I did not look away from him.

He was standing up straight with his arms out just a little, like he was trying to make himself look as big as he could. He stared at me with hard eyes, but I could see the tremor in his jaw. Then slowly he relaxed, and something like a smile spread on his face. "You're a good girl, Zulaikha. More like your mother than you will ever know. And I would be honored for you to go to the school your baba built."

He held out his arms for a hug. I hesitated for a moment, but then felt Malehkah push me toward him. And no matter how I tried to stay angry with him, I felt myself relaxing into his embrace and resting my head against his chest. When we finally took a step apart, I looked up to my father again. "And, Baba-jan?" I asked.

Baba put his hands on his hips. "What is it now?"

"I think I *do* want a chadri." I shrugged. "You know, so the boys will leave me alone on the way to school."

He nodded. "You certainly are growing up, Zulaikha." My father smiled and wiped his brow before he left the room.

✦ ✦ ✦

Up on the roof, a few minutes after the morning prayer, footsteps crunched on the mudstone behind me. Malehkah looked at me with her nose swollen and dark bruises under her eyes.

"Do you need something?" I asked.

"This belonged to your mother. She had promised to teach me to read it, but…" She shrugged as she held out a worn brown leather-covered book. "I brought it up here that night, so the Taliban never found it. Anyway, she would want you to have it."

"Tashakor." My voice was nearly a whisper and my hands shook as I accepted this last piece of my mother.

Malehkah stared at me, but didn't move. There were hundreds of questions I wanted to ask her, but somehow none of them seemed just right. It was silent for a long time. Finally, I had to ask, "Why did you—"

"I was always hard on you... because I felt..." Malehkah swallowed. "I was married off like Zeynab when I was not much older than she was. I had to take care of someone else's children and then my own. And when I looked at you, with the way your mouth used to be..." She touched her own mouth. "Your hopelessness reminded me too much of my life."

Downstairs, baby Safia cried. "There has to be..." Her voice shook. She reached out her hands and gestured at our compound before waving toward herself. "...has to be something better." Malehkah turned and headed for the steps, but she stopped and faced me before she went down. Tears were in her eyes. The baby's cry was turning to a wail. "Something better, Zulaikha."

When she was gone, I pulled my chador tighter

around me against a cold breeze. Dark clouds had blown in and hovered over the eastern mountains. Winter was coming. It would rain soon. I crouched down and looked at the book Malehkah had given me. My mother's book. I could read the faded silver lettering on the worn leather. *Yusuf and Zulaikha*.

When I looked to the sky again, the rising sun burst through the cloud cover in splintering golden-white rays. I hoped it was a message from Allah. A sign to tell me things would get better. That somehow life could be happy – could be filled with something real and lasting and meaningful.

A gentle breeze blew my hair back, and I smiled as I closed my eyes to let the sun warm my face. Then, with my finger, I wrote a single word in the dust: *Inshallah*.

GLOSSARY AND PRONUNCIATION

Afghani (*Afghaanee*) – the Afghan unit of currency

Allahu Akbar (*Alaahu Akbar*) – an exclamation that means "Allah is the Greatest" or "Allah is Great!" Known as the *takbir* in Arabic, the phrase is used in both the call to prayer and the five daily ritual prayers.

Anwar (*Anwar*)

arusi (*aroosee*) – the second stage of an Afghan wedding, a combination of further ceremony and wedding reception, filled with food, dancing, music, and gifts

baba/Baba (*baabaa*) – father

bacha (*baachaa*) – boy

baksheesh (*bakhshish*) – a gift

bale (*baalay*) – an expression meaning "okay, good, yes"

chador (*chaadar*) – a semicircular shawl, often worn as a head covering and held closed in front

chadri (*chaadaree*) – a garment that some Muslim women wear in public. A long veil that rests on top of the head and extends below the knees, with a small mesh screen over the face for sight and breathing. Known in Arabic as a *burqa*.

dastarkhan (*dastarkhaan*) – a large tablecloth spread out on the floor, where food is set out and meals are served

dewana (*daywaana*) – crazy or foolish

Eid (*Eed*) – an Arabic term meaning "festival"; in Islam, commonly used to refer to the holiday of Eid ul-Fitr, which celebrates the end of Ramadan, the holy month of fasting

Gulzoma (*Gulsooma*)

Habib (*Habeeb*)

hajji (*haajee*) – a title of honor for a man who has made the Islamic pilgrimage (the *hajj*) to Mecca

Hajji Abdullah (*Haajee Abdulaah*)

inshallah (*Inshaalah*) – "God willing"

-jan (*jaan*) – suffix meaning "dear," appended to a name as a sign of affection

Khalid (*Kaleed*)

khuda hafiz (*khudaa haafiz*) – goodbye

madar (*maadar*) – mother

Malehkah (*Malika*)

muezzin (*moazin*) – in Islam, one who calls the faithful to perform the five daily ritual prayers. The call itself is named the *adhan*.

muallem (*malim*) – teacher

mullah (*mulaa*) – a Muslim trained in religious law, usually holding an offical position

naan (*naan*) – an oven-baked flatbread, made with yeast

Najibullah (*Najeebulah*)

nikah (*nikaah*) – literally, the wedding contract between a Muslim bride and groom; also used to refer to the ceremony in which this contract is formalized and the bride-price is paid

perahan-tunban (*payraan wa tunbaan*) – the Dari name for a set of clothing consisting of a long tunic over a pair of loose trousers; known in Urdu as a *shalwar kameez*

rafiq (*rafeeq*) – in Arabic, "friend"

rubab (*rubaab*) – a lute-like musical instrument played by plucking; one of the national instruments of Afghanistan

sahib (*saahib*) – a term of respect

salaam (*salaam*) – a common greeting; in Arabic, "peace"

salaam alaikum (*salaam alaikum*) – a common Islamic greeting meaning "peace be upon you"

shahba-henna (*shabi hinaa*) – a party held the night before a wedding, at which the bride's feet and hands are painted with henna

The **Shahnameh,** sometimes known as the 'Book of Kings', is an epic poem describing the founding of the Persian Empire in the area now known as Iran. It was written by the Persian poet Firdawsi (935-1020).

shirnee-khoree (*shirnee khoree*) – an engagement party; literally, "the sweet eating"

tabla (*tabla*) – a drum played with the hands

Tahir Abdullah (*Taahir Abdulaah*)

tandoor (*tandor*) – a clay oven used to bake naan as well as other foods

tashakor (*tashakur*) – thank you

toshak (*toshak*) – a narrow mattress that could be used as either or both a bed and a sofa

wah wah (*waah waah*) – an expression meaning "hooray, congratulations, good for you"

walaikum salaam (*walaikum salaam*) – the standard response to "salaam alaikum," meaning "And upon you be peace"

wudu' (*wu zoo*) – in Islam, the act of cleansing the body before the ritual prayers

Yusuf and Zulaikha – a poem retelling the story of Joseph (Yusuf) and Potiphar's wife, traditionally named Zulaikha. Their story is included in the Holy Quran, the Torah and the Old Testament of the Bible. The excerpts in this book are taken from the version written by the Afghan poet Jami (1414-92).

Zeynab (*Zaiynab*)

Zulaikha (*Zolaiykhaa*)

AUTHOR'S NOTE

I wrote this novel by accident.

At the beginning of 2004, my six years of part-time service in the Iowa Army National Guard were almost over. I planned to teach high school English and write books about kids living the adventure of growing up in the small towns of Iowa, like I had. But just like Zulaikha, I found out that life doesn't always go according to plan. In January, the army called me to active duty, and in late June of 2004, I left America for the first time in my life and found myself transformed from aspiring writer to terrified soldier, in the middle of war-torn Afghanistan.

Based on what I knew about the war from television and from my army training, I had expected my unit's mission to focus on hunting down terrorists – shooting and being shot at by the same kind of monsters who killed so many Americans on 9/11. Instead, as I sweated in a tent at the air base in Bagram, Afghanistan, I was shocked to hear that my unit would provide security for the reconstruction of the country, which had been devastated by many long years of war. Specifically, we were going to be assigned to one of the Provincial Reconstruction Teams (PRTs) stationed at small bases around Afghanistan. These PRTs were designed to help the Afghan people establish schools and improve roads and communications. The army hoped the peace secured by the PRTs could offer Afghans a chance to build a better future for themselves, free of the influence of the oppressive Taliban militias.

To my everlasting shame, I was upset when I heard about my peacekeeping assignment. I remembered the horrible images I'd seen on 9/11, and I blamed the Afghans. I made the terrible mistake of assuming that most of the Afghan people were just like the terrorists. I felt that if I had to be taken away from my home and family, I wanted my chance to make the terrorists pay.

When I reached my station in the western Afghan city of Farah, though, my feelings began to change. Instead of finding American-hating monsters, I met kind people and a lot of smiling, curious children. Afghans offered friendly greetings when we came to their villages. Some of them invited us to dine with them in their homes. A few times, they even helped us dig our Humvees out of the mud when we were stuck. I began to understand the difference between dangerous groups like the Taliban and the typical, peace-loving Afghan people.

After about a month, our first load of mail finally arrived. A package from my wife contained a paperback copy of a children's book by Katherine Paterson called *Bridge to Terabithia*. In a difficult time, when food rations were low and I was feeling very scared and lonely, I read this wonderful story of true friendship. It reminded me of hope and peace and beauty. That same day, I stood at my guard post, looking over the top of the wall that surrounded our tiny compound. Across the street, I saw a little Afghan girl in a dirty dress with no shoes. She dragged a small cardboard box with a piece of string. It was maybe her only toy. As I looked at her and remembered all the Afghan children I had seen, I thought about how much they were like the kids in *Bridge to Terabithia*. They seemed to be full of imagination. They wanted to have fun and friends. A chance to grow up safe.

Finally, I had to admit that all along, I had been wrong about the Afghans. That poor little girl had nothing to do with 9/11. She was not the enemy. She was as much a victim of the Taliban and Al Qaeda as I was. She was more of a victim. At that moment I took my peacekeeping and reconstruction mission to heart.

I began to be as respectful and helpful as I could to the Afghans I encountered. I even volunteered for extra missions that would allow me more interaction with the people, especially if it meant a chance to help the children in some way.

My unit spent our year on duty helping to build schools, providing security for the presidential elections, and handing out toys and candy to Afghan boys and girls. We worked hard to show the Afghans with whom we lived and worked that we were trying to help. We weren't perfect, and I am very, very sorry that we did not help even more than we did, but partly because of our efforts, Farah and western Afghanistan were relatively peaceful in 2004 and early 2005.

As with so much else of my experience in Afghanistan, the girl who inspired the character Zulaikha came into my life by accident. My unit was on a mission to make contact with the elders of a village north of Farah. Our commanders wanted to ask the elders if there was any way the Americans could help improve the village. On this mission, one of the soldiers saw a young girl with a cleft lip. That is, she was born with the two segments of her upper lip not joined in the center. In addition, her nose was disfigured, and her upper set of teeth were badly crooked, some sticking out almost straight forward. These sorts of birth defects occur in the United States too, but American doctors almost always perform corrective surgery early in the child's life. In the case of this Afghan girl, however, surgery would have been hard to get and very expensive. Also, the Taliban who ruled Afghanistan during her early childhood and enforced harsh rules based on their strict interpretation of Islamic law forbade almost all contact between unrelated males and females, and would probably not have allowed a girl to see a doctor anyway.

A short time later, our chief medical officer, a woman not unlike Captain Mindy in this novel, led a second mission to the village to locate the girl and see if we could arrange corrective surgery for her. It wasn't a mission that came down from high command, but one my fellow soldiers and I felt strongly about. After all, if we couldn't at least try to help this girl, what good were we?

Almost miraculously, we found the girl we were looking for soon after our arrival. We tried to be friendly, but given that we rolled into town in armored Humvees, I imagine she was scared when she realized we had come looking for her. Although she was timid and for the most part kept her mouth covered, she had a quiet dignity and a spark of courage in her eyes. The girl's name was Zulaikha. After meeting her, we knew we had to do whatever we could to get her the help she needed.

Since her surgery was not part of our assigned mission from the army, my fellow soldiers and I pooled our money together to buy the taxi fare to a nearby airport for Zulaikha and her uncle, and civilian plane tickets to transport them to our air base at Bagram. An army doctor there volunteered to conduct the surgery. When Zulaikha returned to our outpost in Farah, I was amazed at how much she had changed. Not only were her lip, teeth, and nose completely different, but her demeanor had improved as well. She was still quiet and shy, as anyone might be around strangers, but she no longer covered her mouth with her shawl or her hand. Better yet, she smiled. The last time I saw her, she was riding in the back of one of our trucks, on the way home through our compound's front gate.

Had I not been sent to Afghanistan, I would never have known about her. I thought about all the people back home who might never know about her. Her birth defect was only one of the many obstacles that she would have had to endure in her young life, but she faced it with remarkable strength. To me, she represented all the Afghan girls who are struggling to make better lives for themselves and for their families, and even though she lacked the ability and resources to tell the world her story, that did not mean that it did not deserve to be told. She looked back at me as she rode away, and although she could not hear me or understand my words, I promised her I would tell her story.

Keeping that promise proved more difficult than I at first imagined it would be. I returned to Iowa in June of 2005 and to the high school English classroom a few months later. At the same time, I began studying Afghanistan. Although I had spent a year in Farah, taking extensive notes and many photographs and videos, the Afghan people value their privacy, and I did not know enough about how they lived their daily lives. To compensate for this, I learned all I could about Afghanistan, keeping in touch with a few Afghan friends via the Internet and reading lots of fantastic books. Afghanistan's people and history are fascinating, and I highly encourage everyone to learn more about this great country.

Of course, another problem I had in keeping my promise is that I have never been a girl and I am not an Afghan. Many would say that stories about

Afghan girls should best be told by Afghan girls. I agree completely. I would love nothing more than to read the story of the girl who we helped in her own words. However, the terrible reality is that by some estimates, 87 per cent of Afghan women are illiterate. The Revolutionary Association of Women of Afghanistan (RAWA) recently estimated that up to 99 per cent of women in Farah Province could not read or write. Though progress is being made in Afghan education, too many Afghan girls are simply unable to get their stories out. In spite of this, or perhaps even because of it, I believe it is very important for more Afghan stories to be told, as a greater understanding may foster peace.

I have done my absolute best to be respectful and true to the culture and traditions of Afghanistan. I am grateful for the help of my friend Khalid Siddiq and to my advisors Rebecca Gandum and Fahima Vorgetts for their expert advice. Any remaining errors are entirely my own.

While this is still a work of fiction, the broad outlines of Zulaikha's story are not the only things based in real life. The novel begins in June of 2005 and ends the following September, shortly after Afghanistan's first parliamentary elections in thirty-three years. As mentioned in the text, the people of Farah Province elected Malalai Joya, a woman of great courage who has continued to demand peace, freedom, and equal rights for all the people of Afghanistan up to the present day. The village of An Daral is based on a beautiful mountain valley town called Anar Darreh, and Zulaikha's house is modeled on a compound in Farah where I lived with a small group of my fellow soldiers while we waited for Afghan contractors to finish constructing our base outside the city. The Citadel that Khalid and Zulaikha climb in the story is drawn from a massive ancient castle in Farah, which is said to have been built by Alexander the Great when his army invaded the region around 330 BC Unfortunately, Zeynab's horrible fate, and her last request, were also inspired by true events, and I'll never forget the night when my squad was called out to the Farah hospital to provide what assistance we could to a young and horribly burned Afghan girl.

Finally, I can only hope that readers of this novel will be inspired to want to do more to help the children in Afghanistan. To that end, I recommend readers support Women for Afghan Women, an organization working to secure education and human rights for women in Afghanistan.

I highly encourage everyone to consider donating to this worthy cause. I would also suggest that people interested in helping Afghanistan support Afghanaid, which works for long-term sustainable development in some of Afghanistan's poorest rural areas. The contact information for both these great groups is provided below. Afghanistan faces many challenges, but through the efforts of concerned and caring people around the world, and with the dedication and indomitable courage of Afghans like Zulaikha, a new Afghanistan will rise up from war to a peaceful and prosperous future.

Women for Afghan Women,
158-24 73rd Avenue,
Fresh Meadows,
NY 11366-1024,
USA.
www.womenforafghanwomen.org

Afghanaid,
Development House,
56-64 Leonard Street,
London EC2A 4LT.
www.afghanaid.org.uk

ACKNOWLEDGEMENTS

While all novels, especially first ones, are very special to their authors, *Words in the Dust* means a lot to me because it also represents the fulfillment of a wartime promise. Therefore, I feel a profound sense of gratitude toward all the people who have helped make this book a reality. Special thanks go to my agent, Ammi-Joan Paquette, who gave this novel its first acceptance letter and who connected me to the great people at Arthur A. Levine Books; to my editor, Cheryl Klein, for her belief in this story as well as for her patience and guidance; to Dr Thomas Gouttiere and the people at the University of Nebraska at Omaha Center for Afghanistan Studies for their insights into the Dari language; to Jaime Knipfer, for helping me keep up with checking papers in my classroom and for helping to direct the school play while I worked on this book; to Dr Miriam Gilbert, who helped make me a lifelong English major; to my mother, brother, and sister for their love and support; to the soldiers with whom I served in Farah, Afghanistan, especially those members of the GSC – you know who you are; to Sergeant Matthew Peterson, who taught me

The Cowboy Way, and whose leadership and friendship kept me sane through my time in the war; to Khalid Siddiq, for answering hundreds of questions about Afghanistan; to the wonderful community of the Vermont College of Fine Arts, especially the gloriously talented Cliffhangers, double especially to Mari Talkin, Patti Brown, and Carol Brendler; to all of my VCFA instructors – Rita Williams-Garcia, who was patient and helpful through the first draft, Jane Kurtz and David Gifaldi for their guidance in-between, and Margaret Bechard for getting me to graduation and for asking the important questions; to Katherine Paterson, whose wonderful stories reminded me of beauty and hope during a time when both were in short supply; finally, my deepest love, gratitude, and admiration goes to my wife, Amanda, who always believed in The Dream, even and especially when I didn't. Amanda, you are my life.

TRENT REEDY grew up in Iowa and has always loved
telling stories. He majored in English at the University of
Iowa and paid for his degree by joining the Iowa Army
National Guard, being called to serve in Afghanistan
in 2004. One of the children he encountered in
Afghanistan was a young girl named Zulaikha,
who had suffered since birth from a cleft lip.
A US army doctor gave her corrective surgery,
and Trent was inspired by Zulaikha's quiet courage
and dignity. The last time he saw her, he promised
that he would tell her story. Returning to Iowa in 2005,
he taught English before taking a Master of Fine Arts
degree in writing for children and young adults
at Vermont College of Fine Arts.
He now lives with his wife and their dog Wiggles
in the state of Washington, where he is hard at work
on his second book.

MORE FANTASTIC FICTION FROM
FRANCES LINCOLN CHILDREN'S BOOKS

PAYBACK
Rosemary Hayes

Halima has her whole life to look forward to.
Brought up in a Pakistan village and now settled in London
with her family, her horizons are widening all the time.
She is starting university in London and she has met
a Muslim boy she really likes.

And then she discovers her father's plan – to marry her
to the son of a distant relation in Pakistan who once
did him a favour. Halima is to be the repayment of a debt,
and it's payback time.

"A powerful, moving read."
Irish Examiner

FROM SOMALIA WITH LOVE
Na'ima B. Robert

My name is Safia Dirie. My family has always been my mum,
Hoyo, and my two older brothers, Ahmed and Abdullahi.
I don't really remember Somalia – I'm an East London girl.
But now Abo, my father, is coming to live with us,
after twelve long years. How am I going to cope?

Safia knows that there will be changes ahead but nothing has
prepared her for the reality of dealing with Abo's cultural
expectations, her favourite brother Ahmed's wild ways, and
the temptation of her cousin Firdous' party-girl lifestyle.
Safia must come to terms with who she is – as a Muslim,
as a teenager, as a poet, as a friend, but most of all, as a
daughter to a father she has never known. Safia must find
her own place in the world, so both father and daughter
can start to build the relationship they long for.

From Somalia, with Love is one girl's quest to discover who
she is – a story rooted in Somali and Muslim life that
will strike a chord with young people everywhere.

THE SNIPER
James Riordan

Stalingrad snipers were a legend in their time. Their patience, keen eyes and ruthlessness helped win the Battle of Stalingrad and turn the tide of the Second World War. This is the true story of a teenage sniper recruited in 1942 by Vasily Zaitsev to seek out and shoot German officers. To begin with, the youngster finds it almost impossible to kill, but after a shocking discovery, goes on to 'snap as many as 84 German sticks', and following capture and a daredevil escape, leads a handpicked unit on a hazardous mission – to seize Field Marshall Paulus, the Commander-in-Chief of the invading army.

But this sniper is no ordinary marksman…

"The lyrical opening must be one of the most evocative in children's fiction. Riordan is a consummate teller of tales for young people."
Amazon reviewer

"A powerful and heart-rending story." *School Librarian*

"I for one could not put the book down." *IBBY Link*

BLOOD RUNNER
James Riordan

"Not far now. His lungs are bursting, his legs are as heavy as rocks, his breath rasps in his throat. Every ounce of his body screams STOP! Yet his will is still strong. He has to make it. For his President. For the black people of South Africa. See, if I can do it, so can you!"

Samuel Gquibela's parents and sister die in a bloody massacre. His brothers retaliate by joining the anti-Apartheid movement, with guns and terrorism as their weapons. But Sam decides to fight prejudice in his own way, as a runner. Against all odds – from a poor township childhood to the Bantu homelands, from work in a gold-mine to competing for gold – he focuses his mind, body and heart on the long, hard race to freedom...